DESTINATION
DAINTREE

Destiny in Disguise Series

DESTINATION
DAINTREE

Journey to crocodile country
North Queensland

ANTHONY W BUIRCHELL

Back L2R Isobel, Madeline, Keith, Eva, Burt Front L2R Phyllis, Molly, Max, Rita
The Johnson Family in the Daintree 1932

National Library of Australia Cataloguing-in-Publication
Creator: Buirchell, Anthony W., author.
Title: Destination Daintree : Journey to Crocodile Country North
        Queensland / Anthony W. Buirchell.
Edition: 2nd edition.
ISBN: 9780995424326 (paperback)
Series: Buirchell, Anthony W. Destiny in Disguise series ; 1.
Subjects: Historical fiction, Australian-Queensland. Daintree
        (Qld.)-History--Fiction.

Printed & Channel Distribution
Cover Design- Laila Savolainen
Publishing Consultants/Interior Design- Pickawoowoo Publishing
Group

Publisher
Cric Croc Enterprises, www.criccroc.com
For enquiries, write to: rights and permissions via publisher.
Lightning Source | Ingram (USA/UK/EUROPE/AUS)

Dedicated to Marge Smith (nee Johnson) and her siblings who were in the Daintree with her.

In memory of Madeline, Burt, Eva, Isobel, Keith, Max, Molly, Rita and Phyllis.

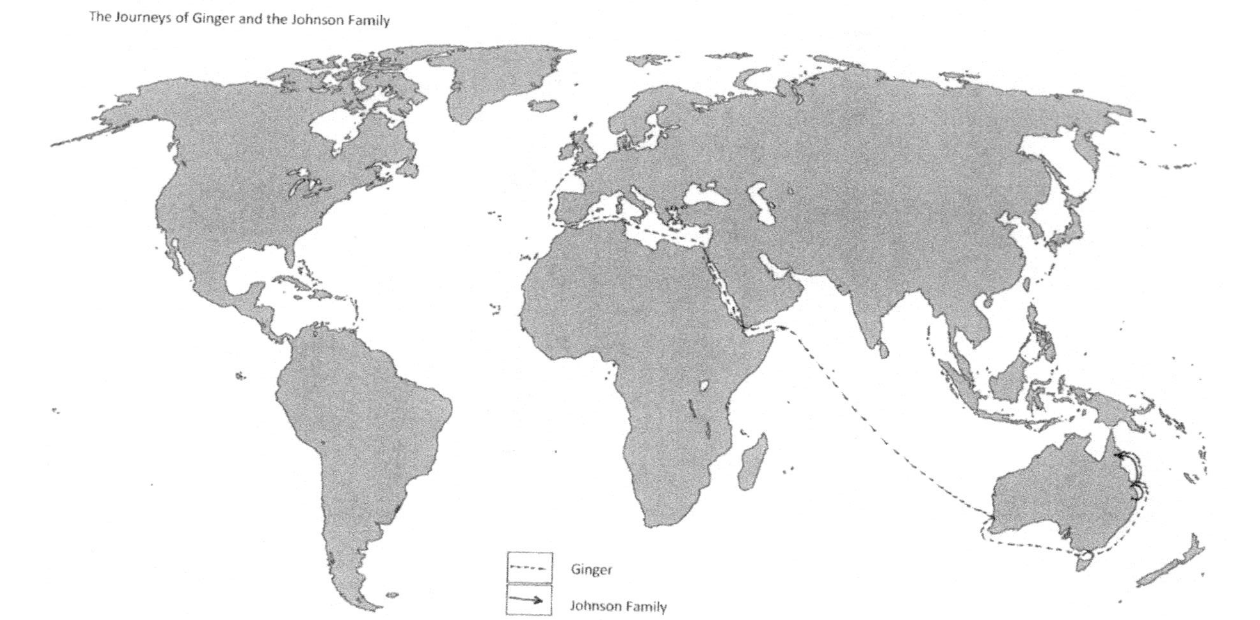
The Journeys of Ginger and the Johnson Family
Ginger
Johnson Family

Chapter 1

England January 27th, 1911

Determinedly the young girl walked along the cobbled road towards her destination. The snow was getting heavier and she could just make out the wooden cross of the church. Once she was there she felt she would be safe.

The Mother Superior and the other nuns would take her in, warm her freezing bones and care for her. They would find her a cup of hot soup and a silver spoon to drink it with.

Her weariness was sapping all her energy and she began to have doubts that she would make the final distance. There was no one around in the small town as they would all be sheltering from the coming storm.

She longed to go back nine months in her life and tell young Master William Blessingham to leave her alone. But the damage was done and she had not resisted in anyway. So he had had his way with her and then kicked her out of the bed. "Get back to the kitchen, woman where you belong and not a word to anyone or you'll be out on the street."

She couldn't afford to be without a job not with the condition her mother was in at that time. Her mother had been poorly ever since she had given birth to Charles her little brother.

What with seven other children to raise and father up and gone it was left to Bess to be the sole breadwinner.

Even that had fallen to nought as her mother became more and more stricken.

In the end Bess had to seek help from the authorities.

Her mother was admitted to a hospital and it was only a few weeks later that Bess received the dreaded news, her mother had passed away.

At the same time as they took away her mother, Bess saw her siblings sent off to a Poor House.

She alone was still able to saviour her freedom. She never saw her family ever again.

Bess was at least thankful that she still maintained her job at Blessingham House, and even more so that Master William had ignored her since the terrifying rape.

Now Bess was fearful for the likely loss of her job because her pregnancy was beginning to show.

Mother had told her all about the wicked ways of men and how they would chance upon a naive young woman and make them do unspeakable things. Bess had thought that these things would never happen to her but now she knew different.

How easy it was all those months ago, for Master William to sneak up behind her while she was making his bed as she was required to do in Blessingham House.

He had startled her by grabbing the ribbon she had tied to keep her black hair from flowing to her waist.

She hadn't heard him coming from the bathroom.

When she turned to face him she was shocked to see that he was stark naked and wet all over. Rivulets of moisture flowed down the golden hair on his chest.

She was shaking from the shock but worse was to come. She could see that his manhood stood stiff amongst the curly red hair of his crotch.

She reached out for her ribbon and in a feeble voice pleaded, "Please sir may I have my ribbon?"

Master William held the ribbon aloft and began to tease, "You can have anything you want, Bess, as long as I can have everything I want."

He played a 'keepy off' game with the ribbon before throwing it to the other side of the bed.

He blocked her way so that finally she crawled across the bed. He then jumped on top of her, rolled her over and began to molest her.

He kept whispering, "I want you and I'm having you. No noise or you lose your job."

He slid his manicured fingers into the hair of her fringe pulled tightly causing her to call out in pain.

"Ssh, you stupid girl or you're in the street."

His strength was too overpowering for her mere

frame. He reached under her dress and slid his hand along her thigh. Roughly he grabbed at her panties and pulled.

Bess heard a tearing noise as the thin cotton ripped. He held the panties above her face to signal his triumph, twirled them on his finger and sent them flying across the room.

He laughed and said, "No more barriers now."

It was not long before he had her legs apart and tried to have his way, pushing and thrusting.

He swore and then laughed, "A lovely little virgin I see, all ready and happy just for me."

Bess was further revolted by his deplorable attempt at rhyming while he raped her.

She felt a stinging pain as her hymen ripped and she knew he had entered her.

The thrusting took on a rhythm, going faster and faster, until she felt an explosive force deep in her nether regions.

William grunted satisfied and rolled away. He swung his legs over the side of the bed and stood up. "Nice, very nice and so willing too," he said.
He found a pair of underpants and pulled these on before going to the wardrobe for the rest of his clothes. He put on a shirt and did up the buttons. He hitched up his riding britches and tightened the belt. He put on a pair of socks and pulled on a pair of riding boots and walked towards the door as if nothing had happened.

"Keep quiet about this little Bess or I'll be back for more and you'll be out on the street."

All the time Bess lay still watching the nonchalant way the master's son went about his dressing. Not once did he show any care for her or remorse for the rape that he had forced upon her.

That was power and it was only in the hands of the rich and strong.

Master William left, closing the door quietly behind himself.

Bess lay still trying to cope with the trauma of rape, knowing she could tell no one of what had just happened.

She sat up and pulled her skirt above her knees and looked down. She saw the unmistakable red of blood and gasped. Mother had told her that if she ever married a man and he made love to her to have a baby then the first time he entered her there would be pain and blood because he was taking her virginity. Now she understood all the motherly talk that she had sat through year before last.

Bess cleaned herself up as best she could using the towel in the bathroom to wipe off the blood. She realised this was not a wise move as it would cause questions to be asked.

She then took the cut throat razor that Master William used to trim his beard with and cut her index finger. Her blood flowed freely over her ivory skin and she washed this away waiting for the wound to seal.

This would give her an excuse to explain why there was blood on the towel.

Next she went back and made the bed and checked for any tell-tale signs of the rape. Luckily the blood that she had spilt was on her petticoat that was well hidden under her dress.

She picked up her torn panties and pushed these down her top, concealing them from prying eyes. She would have to walk home naked beneath her dress.

She finished cleaning the room and went out and down the staircase to the kitchen.

The cook was sweating profusely over an open fire and hardly noticed Bess enter.

"I'm off now Mrs Hampton, will see you in the morrow."

The cook threw a Bess a ruddy faced look and nodded. Bess hurried from the kitchen, threw the towel in the laundry and walked out into the fresh air.

Her groin was aching but she walked strongly away from the huge brick house.

She never looked back fearing the Master William would be upstairs somewhere looking out and gloating.

Chapter 2

Bess had finally reached the cold stone steps of the church.

She felt another spasm strike just above her distended stomach. She felt a sharp kick and smiled, happy to know the baby was still alive.

Now all she had to do was knock on the huge, wooden doors and they would be flung open and help would be at hand.

The snow was increasing in intensity and she pulled the oversized cardigan tightly around her torso. That would keep her heart and the baby warm.

She knew that the storm was on its way with the increase in pitch of the wind as it whistled along the street. The snowflakes were swirling and falling all over the stone entry.

She was exhausted after struggling all the way from her sleeping place under the stairs at the back of the local inn.

She had been homeless and jobless ever since her baby bump became too obvious.

She had to stop work at Blessingham House.

The only saving grace was that she didn't have to

face her mother and tell her that her daughter was out of work, pregnant and destitute.

Bess decided she had to leave her home town and all the gossip that no doubt would ensure.

All the tut, tuts and the speculation as to who the father might have been. All these things she had seen other girls suffer and she was not going to be subjected to any of that.

So she ran away and ended up here in Caterham.

Bess lifted her bare, pale hand and knocked.

She couldn't hear any sound and realised that she no longer had the strength to make the knock loud enough to be heard.

She could now only wait and hope that someone would find her and help her.

She propped herself against the wall at the front of the church and slowly edged her body down. With her bottom less than a foot from the paving she let herself fall the final distance.

She felt the jar through her backbone and was concerned for the baby's welfare.

Her legs were straight and the snow was whipping swirls of white over them.

She pulled her knees up to her chest to get them out of the drifting snow.

Bess again felt the tell-tale kicking in her stomach and knew instinctively that the baby had taken no harm.

The new position was too cramped for her and

within seconds she had to push her legs down again and open them wide.

The spasms were coming at regular intervals and were causing a lot of pain.

She desperately tried to recall what she had seen and heard when her mother had had her little brother Charles.

The birth had begun when Bess heard her mother calling out to her. She had skipped into the bedroom to see what her mother wanted only to find her sitting on the floor with her back against the bed. She had her legs open and her knees pulled towards her chest.

Her mother had said urgently, "My waters have broken you must run and get the midwife."

Bess had looked down to where her mother was pointing to see wetness all over the wooden floor. She was alarmed but set off quickly to find the midwife.

It took some time before the stern, no nonsense midwife could be alerted. "Are you sure that it is time missy. I go rushing off to too many false alarms and this had better not be another," she scolded.

"Yes Mrs Pritchard I've seen the water with my own eyes", said Bess.

Mrs Pritchard gathered her wicker basket of instruments and bandages and set off with Bess.

Bess had to run to keep up with her as she strode out.

As Mrs Pritchard moved along the street the residents called out to her a welcome and sometimes a blessing. The children ran beside her saying hello. She knew many by name and even tousled the hair of a pretty young blond girl of about four.

Bess's mother was still in the same position she was when Bess had run off.

What had changed was the excruciating look on her face. "The spasms are coming quickly now, please help."

"Right," said the midwife taking charge. "You're in a good position and yes the waters have broken.

"Now we must wait for the head to crown. No child can be a king or queen until they have crowned." She chuckled at her own joke.

Bess sat in a corner not knowing what her role in the impending birth would be.

One thing that kept passing through her mind was, "Watch and learn because, as a woman, one day this could be you."

"Hold back and suffer the pains," said the midwife. "You must not push or bear down until we see the head crown. Use too much energy at the wrong time and we'll have trouble and more trouble. Don't want to lose you or the baby now do we?"

The incessant chatter of the midwife was both a blessing and a nuisance to Bess.

She was in a position where she was looking directly at the place where she expected the baby to slide from.

She felt embarrassed and naughty for being here but she was transfixed and thought if she moved and they saw her then she would be in trouble.

At the present neither her mother nor the midwife seemed aware of her.

Suddenly her mother screamed and shook all over. "Hold on. Hold on," said the midwife, "It's nearly here."

Bess watched in fascination as she saw the area between her mother's legs begin to widen and a reddish pink object seemed to ooze out.

"That's it we've got the crowning now push, push, push," cried the midwife.

The head of the little baby appeared and then the body followed sliding gracefully from Bess's mother.

The midwife picked up the slime and bloody covered baby and slipped her finger in its mouth. There was a hiccup sound and then the child starting bawling.

The midwife wiped the child's nostrils and eyes with her fingers and turning it over announced, "Another boy, my dear."

The midwife took two pieces of string from her wicker basket and tied the first around the cord that was shared jointly by mother and child.

Bess had heard her mother talk about this and she'd called it the umbilical cord. It was how the mum fed the bub while it was in the womb.

The midwife tied the second string about an inch further away from the first.

She then took out a pair of silver scissors and snipped through the cord between the strings. She untied the knots and threw the strings into the basket.

"Well that's it," she declared wrapping the baby in a blanket and handing the tot to Bess. "You look after your kid brother and I'll send some of the gawking neighbours in to get your mum in the bed and make her comfortable."

It was the first time that Bess had noticed all the faces staring in through windows and doors.

Now she just wished there was one face looking out for her.

Bess was going through what her mother had gone through except she was all alone. So far no one had come to help her.

She had to stay strong for the baby and she had to remember what to do.

A longer, sharper spasm rocked Bess and she bit her tongue to stop screaming out.

She had to wait for the crowning because she knew she had far less energy than her mother had had when Charles was born.

Bess tried to remember how her mother knew the baby had crowned and realised that it was the midwife who had kept her informed.

She had no one to do the observing so what could she do?

She recalled her own view of the birth and it occurred to her that her mother could have felt the head emerging if she had placed her hands down.

So that's what she had to do.

Bess reached down and felt the wetness all around but no head could she feel.

She had to be patient and she had to forestall the spasms as they came and went.

Bess knew that the crowning was the secret and once it happened then she would use her final strength to push the baby out.

Chapter 3

∽o∽

Australia 27ᵗʰ Jauary, 1911

Twelve thousand miles away Jack Stewart awoke with a start.

The dream was still resonating in his mind but he couldn't quite piece it back together. A flash of a tree trunk splintering as it began to fall, a call of 'Timber' and the searing shock on the side of his head.

Was he awake or what?

He struggled to move and to sit up but he seemed unable to do either.

He thought he heard voices but couldn't make out what they were saying.

Hooves, did he hear the trotting gait of a horse?

The searing heat at the side of his head started again and he called out. What he said he didn't remember. How can you yell that loudly but not remember what you've said?

A hand pressed against his shoulder and a male voice said, "Lay still now Jack you've had a nasty blow to your head."

He lay very still trying to work out where he was and what had happened.

He looked up and saw the sun high above his head.

"It's 12 noon," he thought. "What happened to the last five hours?"

Suddenly everything blacked out.

Burton Johnson was leading the horse that was pulling the spring cart and on the back was a bush stretcher where Jack Stewart's inert body lay.

Walking along at the back were two workmates of Jack Stewart. John Priest was tall and rangy with dark straight hair and Billy Jones, slight but sinewy with a shaved head.

They were both deep in thought trying to work out just how the accident had happened and if there had been anything they could have done to prevent it.

Further back again was Tim Spencer, a Scotsman, pale complexion, blond and unhappy.

Tim had sort a new life in the land down under but found the heat and flies oppressive.

Tim had been working with Burton Johnson felling the last of the redwood cedars that they had marked when they heard a chilling scream, "Man down."

They had dropped their axes at the foot of the partially cut redwood cedar and answered the emergency.

A swift cooee from Burton was followed by a returned cooee.

This gave them direction and distance they would have to traverse before being able to help.

The thick jungle of the rainforest on the side of Mt Warning in the northern part of New South Wales was something to be reckoned with.

The mountain slopes were at 40 degrees and any movement upward resulted in slipping downwards. The best option was to stay on the same level until you were directly below or above where you were headed and then move up or down cautiously.

One had to push through tree trunks, palms, vines, roots and branches avoiding the dreaded stinging nettle and the clinging wait-a-while that were everywhere.

Finally the pair reached a small clearing where they sighted a man in brown overalls desperately cutting the branches from a huge fallen iron bark.

They ran the final 20 yards and Burton called out, "What's happened here?"

The cutter didn't stop but yelled back, "Man down, he's somewhere under these branches. Give me a hand."

As he spoke a second man appeared from within the tangle of branches, vines and leaves.

"Can't find him but he definitely went with the tree as it fell. I saw it with my own eyes."

Burton called a halt and took charge.

His demeanour showed a man who was a leader and one who looked for and found solutions to problems. His tanned skin glistened with perspiration and he was puffing hard after the desperate race through the rainforest.

"First tell us what happened and we'll take it from there."

"Jack Stewart, Billy here and I were cutting on the reverse when the tree suddenly splintered. It took Jack with it and when it crashed he was thrown through the air and has landed somewhere in that mess ahead of us."

"Right," said Burton, "The first thing is to locate him and then work out what to do. No point in wasting energy cutting into branches until we have to.

Tim you go ahead of the tree, down the slope and work back up on the right as you come. Take James here and he works the left. I'll work towards you Tim from up slope and you…" he said then stopped.

"John Priest," the fourth man replied.

"John, you work down to meet Billy. If you find him yell out so we can all see what we need to do to extricate him. Let's move."

It was hard work searching through the debris of the massive tree and all the forest that it had brought down as it fell.

After almost half an hour Tim Spencer called out, "Got a boot over here."

All four men gathered around the place where Tim had found the boot.

By pulling and dragging more branches and undergrowth they were able to reveal Jack Stewart's body. It was still stuck under a large branch which would have to be cut and dragged out of the way.

"Can't tell from here if he's with us or gone to the maker," said Burton.

"John and Billy run back for your axes and get this branch out of the road. Careful it doesn't fall further on to him. Tim and I will work from the other side."

Within twenty minutes of desperate chopping and clearing Jack Stewart's body was able to be lifted clear.

"He's still with us," said Burton and some glimmer of hope showed across his sweating face.

They carried Jack into the clearing and set about examining him. Burton said, "We'll need to carry him out so let's make a stretcher while I fix up this head wound."

The head wound was the sign of a major injury. Burton had not expressed what he could see to the others.

Billy and John rushed off to make a stretcher.

They weren't too keen on working on a dead body because there was no way they believed Jack could survive the blow he copped.

Tim walked away and began to seek out lengths of timber as handles for a stretcher.

Burton wiped the blood away from the jet black hair on Jack's right side. He could see that the skull had been split open. He took his knife from his pocket and carefully cut the hair from around the wound. The more he cut the more alarmed he became.

The wound was the size of a two shilling piece and the skull was missing from this area.

He was staring at Jack Stewart's brain.

Little fracture lines radiated along the skull that was still intact.

Blood kept pulsating from the wound, bright red and trickled on to the leaves below.

Burton felt in his pockets and found a handkerchief. It was still folded into a square so he folded it again and again so that it was a wad. He pushed this onto the ghastly wound and was pleased to see it stem the blood.

He took off his long sleeve shirt and began ripping off the sleeves. He cut these into strips using his pocket knife.

Burton tied the strips around Jack's head first going across the forehead and then around the chin and over the head.

Burton smiled when he realised he had formed a cross with the bandages and thought, "Brother you are going to need the entire Lord's help to get out of this."

John and Billy returned with ropes, hessian bags and a couple of belts. They used their knives to cut the bottom of both bags so that they would form a sock without a toe.

Tim had found two six foot long palm trees that he'd cut and assembled. The three men tied the rope from one pole to the other and then the two belts. This set up a frame and to this they threaded the hessian bags.

The stretcher was laid close to Jack and his limp body lifted gently and placed on the stretcher.

Each man took up corner pole and they began the treacherous descent down Mt Warning. It was thick scrub all the way and slippery underfoot.

They had planned to walk the victim out of the forest so that they would arrive near the spot that John and Billy had left their spring cart that morning.

From there they would tie the stretcher to the cart and get the horse to do the pulling.

At that point Tim was to run across to the other side of the valley and ride his horse back to Tyalgum to raise the alarm and get Dr Sommerville to come along and give Jack better medical help.

He was going to take Burton's horse with him rather than leave it by itself.

Tyalgum was a sleepy little town with barely 25 people living there.

The Butter Factory in the centre of town served the district's main industry, dairying. It was to this building that Tim spurred his horse and at the same time shouting out, "Help, there's been an accident. It's Jack Stewart."

Men came running from various directions and Tim began to fill them in with what had happened.

Doctor Sommerville came walking over from the

hotel where he had been attending a cut hand of one of the patrons. "How bad is Jack, son?" he asked.

"Terrible doctor," replied Tim. "The tree cracked his skull open."

"You say they're coming in on the Limpinwood Track?"

"That's right sir. I'm riding back to help out. We sure could do with your expertise."

"I'll get the light gig right away. Just hold awhile."

While everyone else milled around feeling hopeless in not being able to help one of the young lads from the Butter Factory called to his boss, "Mr Hendrix can I ride out to the Stewarts and alert them as to what has happened? I think Mr and Mrs Stewart would be pleased to be able to ride into Murwillumbah with their son."

"Good thinking son, you have my blessing. Go ride like the wind."

Chapter 4

William John Stewart was Jack's father and he and his wife, Mary Jane had been one of the original selectors in the Bray Creek district.

They had settled on lot 14 and continued to build their family finally stopping at fifteen.

Their off spring was slowly branching out all over surroundings areas.

William John was out riding with his daughter Marion when they spotted a rider going hell for leather towards their homestead. "Seems like someone is in a mighty big hurry father," said Marion.

"Sure does. I think we'd best go down and see what the problem is."

They turned their horses towards the house and spurred them into a gallop. Marion was 24 years old and a spinster. She was an expert horse rider and wore a pair of hand sewn grey culottes. She sat astride the palomino and the pair operated as one.

She was easily first to rein in at the front gate of the house paddock.

Her father reined his white stallion in a good fifteen seconds later.

He dismounted while Marion tied her horse to

the hitching rail next to the bay mare that was sweating profusely.

She walked to her father's horse and hitched that up too.

A young lad came out of the house followed by Marion's mother.

Mary Jane was a small woman, with greying hair. She had been crying and as she walked towards them she was wiping the tears away on her apron.

"What in the dickens is the matter?" demanded William John.

"There's been an accident, sir," said the boy. "Your son Jack has been hit in the head by a tree while he's been tree felling up on Mount Warning."

"How bad is it, did they say? Who's with him? And where's the lad now?" asked William John.

The messenger was startled by so many questions at once. He composed himself and said, "Very bad accident and they are bringing him in along the Limpinwood Track.

They should be in Tyalgum about now.

They are getting Doctor Sommerville to have a look at him and then continuing into the Tweed Cottage Hospital at Murwillumbah," said the boy.

"We'll ride across the creek and come onto the Tyalgum-Murwillumbah road at Hackett's. That way we should catch up or even be ahead of them. Come on girl let's go."

William John and Marion unhitched their horses and mounted. With a wave and goodbye William John set his white stallion on a direct line to clear the creek.

Marion followed seconds later on her palomino.

Mary Jane watched them go and turned to the boy and said, "Thank you for riding out."

He replied, "It was all I could do mam. I sure hope your son is going to live."

Mary Jane watched him ride away and then she knelt on the ground and prayed, "Look after my dear boy, Lord and keep him safe."

The stretcher bearers were moving along carefully and John Priest was leading the horse when Doctor Sommerville's carriage came into sight. They could see he was driving the horse hard by the dust and the swaying of the carriage. He reined in front of them and jumped out. "Is he still alive?" he asked.

"Believe so doctor," said Burton from behind the cart.

Doctor Sommerville untied the bandages and took off the handkerchief. A stream of bright red blood shot out. He quickly replaced the wad and bandages.

"Whoever did the first aid deserves a medal," he said. "I couldn't have done better myself. We need to get the patient along to hospital quick smart if we have any chance of saving him."

"Burton did the tying of the bandages," said Tim Spencer.

The doctor looked from man to man and asked, "Which one is Burton?"

John Priest replied, "The big bloke with red hair at the back. He says he comes from a long line of Danes."

The doctor got back in his carriage and turned it around and trotted back towards Tyalgum.

Tim Spencer waited for the spring cart to go past and he dismounted and led his horse after the others.

There was a crowd in the street of Tyalgum as the stretcher bearing procession trotted through. Everyone was worried and wanted to know Jack's condition.

Doctor Sommerville waited for the horse to turn onto the Murwillumbah Road before he addressed them all.

"Jack is in a bad way. He has a compound fracture of his skull that has exposed his brain. His life hangs in the balance."

Chapter 5

Marion and her father came out on the Murwillumbah Road and looked left and right. Far away in the
distance towards the direction of Murwillumbah they
could just make out several men and a spring cart.

"That'll be them, come on," said William John.

Burton could see the riders coming at full tilt and
hoped they would stop in time.

The horses reined up ten yards from them and Burton recognised William John Stewart as he was one of
the pioneers of the dairy industry out here.

He had done some work for the old man on a property up the Bray Creek valley a few months back.

As for the lovely young lass sitting on the palomino
he didn't know but decided he would like to make her
acquaintance.

"How's my son?" asked William John as he
dismounted.

"Sorry Mr Stewart but he is barely holding on," said
John Priest who had taken over leading the horse and
spring cart.

William John walked to the stretcher and looked
down at his inert son. He saw that he was very pale
and that the bandages around his head showed red just

above the right ear. Jack was clearly unconscious and his breathing laboured.

"Come on we need to get the boy to the hospital there's still 13 mile to go.

Marion will you ride ahead and alert the hospital that Jack is coming. It would be ideal if one of you fellows would go with her. Who's got the most knowledge about the accident and the wound?" asked William John.

"That would be Burton, the redhead," said John. "He's the one who did all the first aid and Doctor Sommerville said it was an amazing effort."

William John turned to Burton and said, "I would appreciate it Burton if you would ride ahead. It will give the doctors a head start on trying to save my boy."

Burton was about to find an excuse for staying with the others when he looked up and caught Marion Stewart's eyes.

She had a peculiar look on her face that was part pain and part expectation.

"Sure I'll go Mr Stewart it will be my pleasure."

Against her feelings and better judgement, Marion smiled slightly.

William John dismounted from his high spirited horse and handed the reins to Burton. Burton mounted easily and set the stallion into a canter with Marion following.

They hardly spoke all the way in until they caught sight of the hill near the Tweed River which they knew overlooked the township.

Burton reined his horse in and set it to a trot. Marion closed the gap and came up beside him. "Do you think Jack will make it?" she asked, trying to get this handsome man to converse with her.

"Sorry mam I can't say. All I know is I tried my best with the first aid."

"We need to carry our message to the hospital as fast as we can."

"These poor horses are almost spent so I suggest we walk them to the top of the hill."

"Thank you for all you've done. Please call me Marion."

They chattered about the weather and some of the people each knew in Tyalgum and Bray's Creek and before they knew it they were hitching the horses outside the main entrance to the hospital.

A young boy was sitting in the shade of a lovely old eucalyptus tree so Burton flipped him a coin and said, "Look after the horses will you lad?"

The boy's eyes lit up as he picked up the sixpence and he eagerly said, "Yes sir."

"You think of everything don't you?" said Marion.

"Not everything but I try to always do my best," said Burton.

Marion followed Burton into the main foyer of the hospital.

She was smitten by his lovely fine, red hair, his thoughtfulness and his impeccable manners.

She was nearly 24 and had never had a suitor so she wondered.

Of course a catch like this was probably already taken, wife and four kids at home.

She had to admonish herself for her thoughts especially considering the gravity of their quest.

A sister approached, all dressed in white, with a red cloak and white veil. She had a pendant watch pinned on her chest, "May I help?"

"We have a badly injured man coming in from Tyalgum that will arrive within the hour. He has been badly injured when a tree he was felling hit him a glancing blow. His skull is fractured and a piece about the size of a florin is missing. You can see his brain tissue and there is considerable bleeding. There are also signs of spider like fractures radiating from the main wound. There may be other problems internally that I couldn't see," said Burton.

The nurse hurried away down one of the long, wide corridors.

Shortly she reappeared with a tall man dressed all in white and a stethoscope was dangling around his neck.

The nurse introduced him as Doctor Bennett and

he asked Burton to go over his story again.

The doctor then walked to a door and opened it before closing it behind him.

Burton made out the large light over a silver, shining bed like structure and fathomed this was the new operating theatre that had only recently been opened.

"Would you both like to freshen up and have a cup of tea while you wait?" asked the nursing sister.

"Lovely idea," said Marion.

As they sat waiting for Jack to arrive they watched a lot of toing and froing into the operating theatre. Some of the people moving around wore gloves and operating caps on their heads.

Burton held fond memories of the hospital because his father, Fritz, had been involved in the Auxiliary. He had been the secretary-treasurer several times and had been involved in fund raising.

Fritz had encouraged all his children Ruby, Burton and Keith to become involved.

Burton recalled in his mind the day long fundraiser that the four had been involved in at the Murwillumbah Show.

They had started by selling cupcakes that the whole family was involved in making.

They then progressed to asking for donations. The amount collected reflected their special approaches to people and of course the worthy cause.

They were collecting to buy one of those x-ray machines that could show you your bones and where they might be broken.

His mind then wandered to the other organisations that his father had been involved in. He smiled to himself when he recalled the disastrous day of the Caledonian Games that Fritz had organised.

The old man had been the secretary and took on the role as the organiser of the games which were based on the Scottish Highland Games. Caber tossing, marching girls, highland fling, hammer throw, you name it they did it.

The funny thing was the fickleness of the weather.

The day had started fine, sunny and cool. A few wispy clouds dotted the eastern horizon and the top of Mt Warning.

People coming through the gates all congratulated Fritz on his choice of day, weather and for his efforts at organising.

By lunch time the crowd was over 2000 and the games were in full swing. Everyone was having the time of their lives.

The cloud formation to the east was closer and greyer than earlier but few people were concerned. The humidity continued to climb making the afternoon uncomfortable to those involved in the more strenuous competitions.

About one o'clock the wind suddenly picked up and the clouds came from two directions.

The downpour saturated everyone as they ran for cover. The rain set in and completely ruined the rest of the day.

Fritz was heartbroken.

He was however given numerous accolades in the days that followed as people appreciated his tireless work in organising the Murwillumbah Caledonian Games.

Finally they heard shouting outside and picked up the unmistakable voice of William John Stewart calling for help.

Burton called out to the nurse on duty, "They are here can you send out a stretcher?"

She walked off briskly and seconds later two orderlies ran out carrying a new red and white stretcher.

"It is certainly better built than our bush one," thought Burton.

A few minutes later the orderlies came back carrying Jack on the new stretcher. They took him straight into the operating theatre.

Now the waiting began.

Chapter 6

Bess's life hung in the balance too outside the Caterham Catholic Church.

She felt down to her crotch again and this time realised that some of the wet was turning to ice.

The fingers of her left hand were stiff with cold.

She knew she was running out of time fast.

She also knew she had one last chance to push the baby out and keep it alive.

Her mother's final spasm had made her shake all over and the midwife knew the sign because she had begun to urge her to push.

Could Bess stay alive long enough or were they both going to perish?

She wondered again why the nuns hadn't appeared outside to check if there were any people seeking their love and care.

Suddenly everything started at once.

Bess felt a spasm begin in the small of her back and rush viciously towards her pelvic region.

At the same time Bess reached with her weakening left arm to feel for the head.

Then she began to shudder all over.

Her fingers felt something hot and round. She couldn't believe it, the head was coming out.

She mustered all her strength for one last push.

The baby slid out and she felt its hotness slide along her arm.

Bess reached down with her right arm and picked the child up. She pressed it towards her left breast and it muzzled towards the nipple and began to suckle.

She pulled the cardigan she was wearing over the child to keep it warm.

Then she felt the umbilical cord and knew it was still attached to her and the baby. She knew it should be tied off and cut but she couldn't muster and more strength.

She cuddled the warm little body and then she knew no more.

At exactly six in the morning Sister Veronica opened the latch on the door to the Caterham Catholic Church and swung it open. A frigid breeze struck her pale face and she shivered. She propped the door open and turned to do the same to the other door when her hand flew to her mouth.

"Oh Lord," she said and blessed herself once and then again. "What has happened here?"

Lying on the freezing cold, stone steps of the church was the body of a young woman. She was so still and looked frozen. Sister Veronica bent down and touched the young woman's face and recoiled when the coldness struck her.

She stood and ran back into the church calling,

"Mother Superior come quickly we have a body on our front step."

Mother Superior was lighting candles at the altar and she stopped and hurried towards Sister Veronica.

"Sister Veronica please calm yourself and be quieter please. Now what are we so concerned about?"

Mother Superior was aghast at the sight that met her eyes.

The young girl had sat down and died on the door step. No one was there to help her.

There was blood frozen all the way down the steps and onto the path.

Mother Superior suddenly grasped what had happened. "Oh the poor girl she's had a miscarriage and died in the night."

Mother Superior knelt beside Bess's stiff body and began to pray.

Then she heard a noise, it was so soft at first then she realised it was a baby crying. She peeled back the Bess's cardigan to reveal a tiny baby still attached to the mother by the umbilical cord.

The midwife had done all she could for the infant and the undertaker had stretchered away Bess's body.

"I'm sorry Mother but you now have full responsibility for our new arrival. My job is done so I will be off."

Mother Superior looked loving at the tiny infant and said, "What life and what future awaits you my little one? Already you have survived more than anyone could ever imagine. I hope you grow up to be loved by the good Lord and by everyone you meet. I pray that you find a loving family to take you in."

She held the tiny baby up to the light and seeing it reflect off his almost bald head said, "I do declare that this one will be a red head when he grows up."

Mother Superior spoke to Father O'Halloran and they decided to send out word to the Caterham Catholic flock to see if there was a wet nurse available to take care of the child.

Mrs Penny Mooreland came forward and so the new baby was taken care of.

At the age of 11 months the baby was transferred to the crèche in the Caterham Orphanage.

Mrs Mooreland was sad to have to hand him over as she had formed a special attachment to him but the rules were the rules.

At the Orphanage he was registered as George Whittaker. The name had come from a family friend of Mrs Mooreland who had died several years ago in a boating accident.

As he grew his shock of red hair became his signature.

The orphanage was run along strict lines and every

child there soon learnt all about hard work, discipline and starvation.

Chapter 7

Jack survived his shocking accident due to the skills of the doctors and nurses at the Tweed Cottage Hospital in Murwillumbah.

They had to clean the wound over and over to ensure nothing could remain that might cause an infection. Then they inserted a silver plate to hold the skull together and to protect the exposed brain tissue.

Rest and recreation was the order of the next five months.

By the time Jack was finally told he could go home he was ready to scream from pure frustration.

Jack Stewart was welcomed home by a gathering of friends and relations at the Stewart homestead. It was evident to all that Jack would never be strong enough again to wield an axe or plough a field.

It was also clear that his brain had been damaged by his accident as his left side did not function as normal causing him to limp.

He was presented with a camera that he was to find most useful for his future endeavours. He not only learnt to use it but also taught himself to process the photographs that he took.

Marion did not see Burton for some time after they parted at the hospital.

She kept a sharp look out for him but he was back in the forest cutting trees.

She said a little prayer to try to keep him safe each evening before retiring.

Rose, her sister noted a change and asked, "Are you alright Marion, you seem so pre-occupied lately? You seem like a woman who has a secret lover."

"Don't be so crass, Rose, it's Jack that I keep worrying about even though the doctors say he will pull through."

Several months after Jack's accident Marion was riding her palomino Pixie, along the Limpinwood Road with Rose when ahead she saw four men fencing.

She thought of asking them for a donation for the church that her family and others were going to build in Tyalgum.

This had been her mission for the past five years.

She and her sisters were sent out often to visit all the farmhouses from Murwillumbah, Tyalgum, Bray's Creek, Pumpenbil, Uki and Chillingham.

Many miles ridden and many pounds collected. Hopefully the new church would soon be built and the Stewarts would get their home back again.

As she neared the men her heart skipped a beat and she whispered absently to her companion, her sister Rose, "See the redheaded man digging the holes, that's the Burton Johnson who helped Jack when he had his accident?"

She was not expecting a reply as she should not have been ogling strange men.

Mother and her father would not approve of such unchristian behaviour.

She was shocked to hear a reply that was somewhat crude, "I saw him first!"

As they drew level with the workers it was clear that Burton was doing all the work while the other three were smoking and joking.

Burton had his shirt off and his bulging muscles were accentuated by the redness of his skin and the streams of perspiration that ran this way and that across his bare skin.

"Hello my pretties?" called one of the men and he took off his straw hat and bowed extravagantly from the waist.

The other two chortled and tugged their forelocks.

"Englishmen," thought Marion, "and not very couth by the way they were trying to act."

Burton Johnson was working hard digging a hole for the strainer post as they had reached the corner of the paddock. This hole had to be deeper and wider than the others and the post was longer and thicker. The post had to take the strain of all the wires from both fences that met at this point.

He seemed to be so engrossed in his work that he

had not heard the ladies approach and the banter of the men was so incessant he had tuned out a long time ago.

One of the men moved to block the path of the horses and Marion had to rein in Pixie before she asked politely, "Excuse us please we wish to make our way unimpeded to the Fogarty farm."

Burton stopped digging and looked up as he had recognised the voice.

He saw Marion, who was wearing a light pink dress with matching bonnet sitting side saddle on her horse.

She was trying to smile but beneath the exterior he felt a touch of fear.

She was not used to being stopped by ruffians and she was clearly displeased.

Burton stepped across, moved his mate aside and apologised, "Marion Stewart please to see you once again. How's your brother Jack going?"

"Burton it is wonderful to meet you again. Jack's doing quite well thank you. May I introduce my sister, Rose."

"Nice to make your acquaintance, Miss Rose. Sorry to hold you up. I'm sure you have important business at the Fogarty place. Please go on your way I'm sure Charlie Smith here was only jesting," said Burton.

Marion and Rose urged their horses forward and cheerily offered a thank you.

Burton called a cheerio and they rode on.

Rose let out a sigh of relief and said, "Burton eh? How do you know him, he's gorgeous and such a gentleman. As for the other fellow, what a common name Smith is, who would want to marry one of those?"

Marion had already decided in her own mind that she had finally found her match.

For too long she had toiled on the farm and watched sister after sister find a man, marry them and go off to produce babies and have a happy life. Now it had to be her time as she was fast approaching twenty five and being called a spinster."

On the way back from the Fogarty's, Marion slowed where Burton and the others were finishing the wiring of the new fence.

She called to him from a distance and he left the group and walked towards her.

"I would like to extend an invitation to you on behalf of my mother and father. They would like you to come to dinner one night."

Burton took off his hat and scratched his red hair and wiped the perspiration from his brow while he contemplated a reply.

"That would be a pleasure I would like to take up. Of course I would also hope that you two lovely young ladies would be there as well?"

Rose began to giggle and blushed, Marion said, "Most certainly. What evening suits?"

"Tomorrow would be fine as we will have finished the fencing by then."

Mary Jane and William John were pleased to get the news from Marion that Burton Johnson would be coming to dinner.

They would then be able to thank him for the miraculous first aid he had administered to their son Jack.

They also were encouraged that Marion had made a formal approach to a man at long last. Hopefully this might develop into something serious.

The courtship of Burton and Marion started slowly as one would expect.

Burton was at his courteous best in the presence of Marion and her parents. He was pleasant, well-mannered and never overstayed his visits.

After nearly ten days of this impeccable behaviour Marion was becoming alarmed and frustrated.

She was publicly quiet, reserved and conservative but privately she had a sexual hunger that few would have understood. She pined for the moment that Burton would hug her, that he would kiss her, that he would make love to her. All of these things seemed remote as he played the perfect suitor.

Marion was waiting patiently for Burton to arrive so that they could go for a walk along Bray's Creek. This was a pleasant outing and they enjoyed each other's company even though little was said.

Marion decided that she had to take the initiative and do something to hopefully arouse in Burton some passion.

As they walked she kept moving close to him and accidentally on purpose touching his arm. He moved away to maintain personal distance.

Finally, frustrated, Marion pushed him in the side. Burton was not expecting a shove of any kind and was caught off balance. He tripped and fell, rolling down the creek bank and into the water.

He sat up with a look of thunder across his face.

Marion gasped, thinking she had spoiled every chance she ever had.

She expected him to charge off to the homestead, mount his horse and ride into the sunset never to be seen again.

She started to apologise, "Oh. I'm so sorry Burton. I never meant for you to fall in the creek."

Burton sat up, retrieved his hat and started to laugh. The sound of his laughter filled the surrounding creek and echoed into the rainforest.

He stood up and pointed at Marion and said, "I'll give you a minute start for the barn. If I catch you before then I'll give you a good spanking," he winked and started counting.

Terrified Marion hitched up her long dress and ran.

It was over 100 yards to the barn and her dress restricted her running.

She could hear Burton's heavy footsteps gaining on her.

She reached the barn and ran inside searching for somewhere to hide.

She was also hoping he'd changed his mind about the spanking.

Marion made for the stooks of hay that were piled against the back wall and was about to jump in amongst them when Burton caught her. He grabbed her arm and spun her around. For some odd reason she loved the forceful way he was handling her. Burton twisted her right arm behind her back and held her close.

He was breathing heavily and the hotness on his body aroused her.

She leant forward trying to work out how to bring her lips to his but he was so much taller and he remained upright.

Suddenly he let her go and stepped back. "I'm terribly sorry Marion, whatever am I thinking. Please forgive me for my uncouth ways."

Burton was visibly shocked by his behaviour and Marion sensed that she was about to lose him forever.

She grabbed at his arm and wanted to say, "Have your way with me, I'm all yours!"

Instead she weakly said, "You're all wet. We need to get you out of those clothes."

He stopped short in his bid to escape and an odd

look came over him. He turned back and grinned.

Unintentionally she had used the right words to literally break the ice. "You can take my clothes off if I can take yours off!" he said huskily.

Their love making was like nothing either of them had expected. Marion had a sexual appetite that even shocked her. Once aroused she fervently enjoyed herself and Burton.

Burton could not believe what was happening.

Here was a woman who knew an assortment of tricks, with her body. He had heard other men talk about sex in a crude way but this was unbelievably sensual and full of desire.

She had a magical way of keeping them both at the point of no return without tipping either over.

At last they could no longer hold out and were overwhelmed with happiness when they finally came together.

Spent, they lay in the straw and dozed.

Burton was awakened by the sound of William John and Frank approaching the barn.

They were talking loudly as if they were some distance apart so Burton thought it would be a minute or two before they appeared.

He woke Marion and held his hand over her mouth and whispered a ssh in her hot ear.

She realised that her father and brother were

approaching the barn and that she was in a state of undress.

She caught on and realised the urgency in Burton's voice. "Take your clothes and go to the back. I'll stall them while you get dressed. Then go back to the house. Tell your mother what happened at the creek and that I'm waiting in the barn to dry off. I'll catch up with you later."

Marion disappeared and Burton pulled on his underwear.

"Hello there Mr Stewart," he said as William John appeared at the barn door.

"What the dickens is going on here? Where's Marion?" asked William John.

Frank appeared, took one look at the near naked Burton and began to chortle.

"Nothing to worry about sir," said Burton. "Marion and I were walking along the creek and I slipped and fell in. Silly me. Anyhow Marion suggested I make for the barn to dry out. She of course, not wanting to make me feel embarrassed, said she would go back to the house and tell her mother what had happened."

"Oh how disappointing," said Frank. "I thought you and Marion might have decided to consummate your relationship."

"Yes I thought we might have had a wedding too," said William John. "How much longer do I have to wait Burton before I hear the good news?"

Chapter 8

George Whittaker was growing into an infant.

The crumpled up baby look was smoothing out and the red hair was now like a bushfire flaring into the sky.

The wet nurses had been endeared by the chubby little fellow and the heartbreaking story of his birth. They chattered among themselves but played mum if the manager came by.

At twelve months George was transferred to the crèche section of the orphanage and that was a sad time for all the nurses who had fallen in love with him.

The people in the crèche were not as sympathetic towards the little ginger haired boy nor did they have neither time nor inclination to be kind.

Their job was to turn the child into a hardworking, educated teenager so that he could be taken away by rich, adopting parents. The more money they paid the better off was the orphanage.

Nothing more and nothing less would do.

Of course this would cost the orphanage considerably as he grew, so every opportunity was taken to reduce the cost.

Meals were frugal and only twice a day, children were washed every second day and lights were not turned on in the dormitories.

George suffered each day without understanding what his lot entailed until he reached his fourth year.

It was from here on that his memory would start to record episodes of his life. The episodes that were etched into his mind were those that caused the most angst and trauma.

His very first memory was finishing his breakfast of gruel and still feeling hungry.

His tiny stomach growled and he felt faint so he reached across the table to the boy on the other side and said, "Are you going to eat your bowl?"

"Can't," came a feeble reply. "I'm too sick."

The pale faced boy looked down as he pushed the half empty bowl across the table.

George had to kneel on his bench and reach across to retrieve the food but in doing so he raised his mop of red hair above the crowded masses.

Suddenly, there was a bellow from one of the men supervising, "What's going on over there? Sit and don't you dare move."

He was already committed to taking the bowl so in one movement George grabbed the bowl and sat on his bottom.

He hungrily began to wolf down the thick porridge.

A stinging blow to the side of his face pulled him up short.

As he searched for the protagonist he felt another stinging blow across the fingers of his right hand.

"How dare you steal Johnnie's food you little beggar. I'll teach you to break the rules. Get the bucket and mop and scrub the dining area until it shines," yelled the supervisor.

This was how his life would pan out with severe discipline given out whenever and wherever. No one in the orphanage was exempt from these thrashings.

When he reached six he was required to attend learning classes.

This was the best time of George's short life.

He was a clever scholar and quick to pick up on things.

His reading, writing and arithmetic advanced quicker than his other classmates.

He was still under the stern discipline regime and got his fair share of the cane for infractions but at least he was able to enjoy his growing knowledge and skills.

In 1921 he was moved to the senior section where the children were required to take on more responsibilities and learn important skills that would get them ready to be adopted by adults in the outside World.

These people were searching for labourers, maids and sometimes children to call their own. The latter were few and far between and those children selected by these parents were truly blessed.

George was now ten and most of his fellow inmates

and the staff had started to call him Ginger.

His supervisors were wary of him as there was a belief that red-haired males were likely to be rebellious. It was something to do with the connotations of red and fiery plus Irish and red hair.

Whichever way anyone looked at it George was still a target for the severe discipline that was meted out.

At ten all the orphans were sent out to the court yard to begin their outdoor training. This meant lining up at the huge wrought iron gates that separated the building from the five acres of land out the back.

At this point the supervisor would assign each child to a work detail and hand them an implement.

On his first assignment George was put on garden work and given a hoe.

He was then lined up again with about a dozen others and marched to the garden.

Here he was surprised to see an assortment of vegetables growing from neatly laid beds. Each bed had a different vegetable growing in it. There were broad beans, peas, carrots, turnips, cabbages and potatoes.

The leader who was one of the older boys showed each child how to use their implement.

George soon got the hang of chipping away at the vacant soil with his hoe turning over the top six inches and removing any weeds.

His biggest challenge was to make sure that only

weeds came out and not vegetables. The latter indiscretion would result in a hiding.

Day after day the outdoors activities continued as did the two hours of study.

George was pleased that he was getting a rounded education.

His big query in his own mind was where was this all leading?

Most of the children were ready for adoption by the time they reached their eleventh birthday. At that stage in their lives they were required to do etiquette training whereby they were taught manners and the way to conduct oneself as a lady or gentleman in society.

You had to be chosen to do this training and it generally meant that it was considered you would make a fine adoptee.

George saw mate after mate selected and after a few months their beds were made but vacant. He was never approached so he continued to work hard, learn with enthusiasm and take his beatings like a man.

In the outdoors he was learning a number of new skills that he hoped would stand him in good stead with whoever would sponsor him.

He loved the gardening and watching the seeds he planted raise their green shoots to the sky and the way they grew and produced the vegetables. He would secretly pick some of the produce and eat it whenever the supervisor wasn't looking.

Chapter 9

Four months after Burton and Marion had their roll in the hay they were engaged and two months after that, on the 14th June, 1912 they were married.

Of course, Mary Jane and William John were keen on the redheaded Dane who had not only swept their daughter off her feet but had saved their son Jack's life.

"The good Lord works in mysterious ways," said Mary Jane.

The good part for them was she was now off their hands and they could look forward to more grandchildren.

Burton and Marion were married by her father, William John, who was a lay preacher.

The ceremony took place in the church that was in the old part of the Stewart Homestead and was attended by over 65 people. Most of them were relations of Marion as she had 14 other siblings including her twin brother Hersee.

Burton's mother, Phoebe and his father, Fritz attended.

His sister Ruby was a bridesmaid and his young brother, Keith, was his best man.

William John welcomed his new son-in-law with open arms and open house.

The Johnsons were to stay in the Bray's Creek house while they raised their family.

A few months later, Marion was so excited when she confided in her mother that she had missed her monthly period. "That means I'm going to have a baby doesn't it?"

"One would assume that to be true and that's what happened to me each time I became pregnant," replied Mary Jane, "That's not always true for everyone. You will just have to wait for a while longer and then you can tell Burton and everyone else the news. In the meantime let's keep this between us."

Madeline was born on the 22nd March, 1913 at the Tweed Cottage Hospital.

Burton had taken Marion on the long ride from Bray's Creek in the gig.

Along the way they reminisced about the day they took Jack into medical help.

"It's amazing how well he has progressed when you consider he had a piece of his skull gouged out by that tree," said Marion.

She tried to move to a more comfortable position but the baby kept digging her in the ribs.

"I'd agree with that. The moment I saw that wound and looked directly at his brain tissue I thought he would die. To come through the journey on the stretcher, lying on the back of the spring cart and then the operation to insert the silver plate, I don't know how he did it," said Burton.

The horse slowed as it trotted across the bridge over the Tweed River. It must have sensed that it had to haul the cart and its two passengers up the steep hill to the Tweed Cottage Hospital.

Burton, always so considerate called the horse to whoa. He climbed out and walked to the horse and led it up the steep incline.

It was always the hardest part of the journey and Burton wondered as to why anyone would perch a hospital so high on a hill.

Burton hitched the horse and helped Marion get off the gig.

Her pregnancy was clearly evident and two nurses came hurrying out to assist.

"Welcome, Marion," greeted the shorter of the two and Marion recognised her as the one who had been on duty when they had arrived to bring the news of Jack's accident.

As Burton and the two nurses assisted Marion through the doors into the wide foyer Burton felt a cold shiver run up his spine.

He hesitated for a moment and then shrugged off the feeling.

It would return to him later when he left the hospital.

He hoped it wasn't a warning that something was going to happen to Marion or the baby.

Three weeks later Burton was called back to the hospital to pick up Marion and Madeline and to take them home.

His introduction to the baby was one of immense joy.

He was so proud of Marion and his lingering kiss showed how much he loved his wife.

Burton helped mother and child into the gig and set the horse on its journey home.

As he rounded the corner to begin the descent something made him look back at the hospital. The two nurses were standing waving and the scene was a happy one but for Burton something was not right. It was as if the omen he had sensed at the time he brought Marion to the hospital had grown stronger

"Whatever did it mean?"

Mary Jane and William John were delighted with their daughter and doted on their new granddaughter.

Madeline was a perfect baby for a first and Marion was able to feel that having children was easy.

She did however scald her mother one day for using the shortened form of Madeline. "She is not mad so I will beg that you call her Madeline, mother, not Maddy.

Burton had been busy with jobs around the district and he was getting a fine reputation as an honest and hardworking young man. He was always in demand.

William John had taken him aside not soon after he married Marion and told him he would guarantee a job if he ever needed work.

So all in all Burton was employed all the time and his bank account slowly crept up.

He often rode to his father's property at Dunbible, just to the east of Murwillumbah and on the Tweed River. The dairy farm had 40 head of cattle and was doing well. His young brother Keith helped his father, Fritz to keep the enterprise going.

Today was sunny and clear when Burton rode through the gate and hitched his horse to the milking shed.

Inside he could hear the noises of a milking shed in full operation.

Burton walked through the doorway and Keith called out, "Welcome Burton, pull up a stool and help us finish off. The old man is letting the last of the cows out into the paddock."

Burton walked over to his younger brother and saw that he had gained some weight since they had last met.

Keith had been a skinny, weedy little kid although he was quick and wiry. He slapped him on the back in a brotherly greeting. "I'm always happy to help out."

Fritz, the boys' father, came back in and briefly acknowledged Burton's presence.

"Still not happy with me is he?" he directed the question to Keith who shook his head.

"He'll get over it eventually. At least mum is on your side," said Keith.

Burton and Keith finished the separating of the cream and skim milk before making their way to the homestead.

Phoebe, their mother, was in the kitchen and as they entered the smell of freshly baked bread caught their attention.

"Yummy, that smells lovely," said Burton.

Phoebe turned around and rushed into Burton's arms. He gave her a hug thinking at the same time how short she was. She was even shorter than Marion but wider at the waist.

"How are you my dearest boy?" she asked.

"Well mother and too busy. I never get a rest."

Phoebe rushed on, "And Marion and the baby? Why haven't you brought her over to visit us we see so little of you all these days?"

"Just trying to keep the peace that's all," said Burton and pointed out the kitchen window where he could see his father advancing towards the house.

"Oh he's changing little by little. I keep mentioning Madeline and he says you don't want him to be her grandpa, but I tell him that that's not true," said Phoebe.

"It's definitely not true, we'd love to visit and we'd love him to be holding her and playing games. She's a real beauty too," said Burton.

Fritz entered the kitchen and sat in his chair at the head of the table.

Burton noticed he had lost weight and was slimmer than he could ever recall. His reddish hair was a reflection of his own. It was the Danish forefathers who had passed on their Viking features and hair colouring.

He looked at Keith and saw his dark brown hair and that matched his mother's.

Keith was talking about the milking and how pleased he was that the Butter Factory had increased the price of cream to 13 pence.

"That will make you a millionaire dad!" and he laughed.

Fritz tried to keep a serious demeanour but the joke broke the exterior and he chortled.

"And when that happens I'll sell up and buy me a mansion on the South Bank in Brisbane."

That comment set them all off laughing. None of them could ever imagine Fritz living in the big city. He was a country man, born and bred in Daylesford, Victoria then farmed in northern New South Wales before moving to Dunbible.

"When are you going to bring that delightful young wife and my granddaughter over, Burton?" asked Fritz.

The question threw Burton and he could only sit and stare. He wasn't even sure he heard the question maybe he'd thought it up in his own mind.

"Cat caught your tongue has it boy?" Fritz continued.

Burton realised just in time that this was as close a

compromise that his father was likely to offer. "Sunday if that would fit into the busy life you all have."

"Sunday it is," replied Fritz and he stood up and took his cup of tea out onto the verandah.

Burton was about to follow when Phoebe whispered, "Let him be. That was a huge step now he needs time to digest it along with the tea."

Keith and Phoebe laughed and Burton sat still stunned by his father's change towards him.

Burton mounted his horse and said his goodbyes to his mother and brother. He trotted the horse out the gate and along the road before encouraging it into a canter.

He would return Sunday and hopefully his father would welcome his family with open arms.

The family of Burton, Marion and Madeline had arrived in time for Sunday lunch. They had been welcomed by Phoebe, Keith and Burton's sister, Ruby.

Fritz arrived a few minutes after everyone had sat at the dinner table.

Madeline melted Fritz completely.

Phoebe, with the help of Ruby, had set the table for a three course meal. She had found her best silverware and best cutlery. It looked more like a Christmas dinner than an everyday September dinner.

Phoebe had included hand sewn green serviettes

and little cards shaped into a baby. "Thought it would be nice to celebrate Madeline's first meeting with her other family," she had explained.

Marion greeted her father-in-law cheerfully then strategically placed Madeline on his knee.

Madeline did the rest. She smiled and giggled and kicked her stubby feet. Then she took hold of his thumb, popped it in her mouth and began to suck on it.

"Big kisses for grandad, oh she loves you to bits," said Marion.

Fritz couldn't keep pretending to be unhappy and was soon joining in, and between him and his grand-daughter they were the life of the party.

The three hours that Burton, Marion and Madeline spent at Dunbible would be remembered as the happiest ever.

As they were saying their goodbyes Burton took Keith aside and said, "Are you getting treatment for those pimples that you've developed?"

Keith might have been angry at such a question but coming from Burton he knew it was a genuine concern. His answer would prove to be prophetic, "It's alright Burton, they won't kill me."

Burton went back to his farm labouring jobs, Marion to her mothering, Madeline to her babyish ways and before long they had almost forgotten the wonderful hours they had spent with Grandpa and Grandma Johnson along with Aunty Ruth and Uncle Keith.

Chapter 10

Keith was still at school as he was a very bright student. He was in his final year and the study expected, along with the long hours on the farm was slowly exhausting him.

When he reached high school in Murwillumbah he joined the cadets. He loved the idea of marching around with a 303 over his shoulder, shooting practice at the rifle range and bivouacs.

As he moved through the high school years he also moved through the ranks as a soldier. He was now an under officer and a very popular one at that.

His commanding officer, one of his teachers, could not have been more proud of the way Keith presented himself and the fine example he set for his fellow cadets.

Fritz had arranged for a photograph to be taken of Keith in his khaki uniform. He had turned to Jack Stewart to bring his Brownie over and to take the portrait. The picture showed Keith standing to attention, in his khaki uniform and black boots polished to shining.

Fritz put the photo in the top drawer of his dressing table because the boy's pimples showed across his face and there was a blemish of light showing just above the slouch hat.

Fritz had mentioned the light to Phoebe saying, "Looks like a halo and shouldn't be there."

Keith had seen the photo and was equally appalled with the way the acne showed. The light blemish was not to his concern.

One morning in late September, Keith woke up with a pain on the nape of his neck. He wasn't overly concerned as he had been wrestling at cadets to strengthen his muscles and learn hand to hand combat techniques.

He jumped out of bed and looked in the mirror. There was a red area where he felt the pain and wondered if one of his protagonists had used too much pressure on the area as it looked like a thumb print.

He dressed quickly and went off to breakfast. As usual he had a long, busy day ahead. At school he kept rubbing the painful area on his neck.

By night time he noticed that the red area had a yellow centre. "Another damn pimple," he said. He looked in the mirror and saw numerous others across his face. Some were forming, others healing and many red raw where he had squeezed them.

The next morning when Keith awoke he was in agony from the pimple on his neck.

As a budding soldier he was not going to be a wimp so he told no one.

He went off to the milking shed to begin the day's work.

On his way along the path he automatically reached to the pimple on his neck. He placed his index finger on one side and his thumb on the other and squeezed. The pain was more intense and he stopped.

He looked at his fingers for the tell-tale sign of red and yellow that indicated he had burst the pimple but there was nothing. The pain continued.

Keith believed from experience that if he got the puss out then the healing process would begin and the pain would soon subside.

He tried again.

The pimple remained but the pain was excruciating so Keith decided it best to ignore the troublesome spot.

Milking was a chore he did but it wasn't enjoyable.

He would rather have marched around the parade ground in full kit and the heavy Lee Enfield 303 across his shoulder. At least he felt important and held a position that made others look up to him.

The Boer War was a distant memory and the last that Australians fought in.

The World had been pretty quiet since then and Keith sorely wished something would fire up. He would proudly go and fight for his King and country. He would go in as a commissioned officer given his cadet experience and the rank he had attained. He would command a platoon of men and they would be the best.

He reached the cow shed and began preparing the

stall for the first cow. He found the stool and added some chaff to the feed box before opening the gate.

The first cow was well rehearsed and trotted in to push its nose deep into the chaff. She snuffled and snorted as the chaff was pushed up her nostrils.

Keith said, "Come on old girl move across so I can put you in the yoke and tether your hind leg. He pushed on her flanks and she obliged.

He felt wetness on his right hand and looking down realised he had wiped it in cow dung that was splashed on the cow's flanks.

He flicked his hand to get rid of the smelly mess and at the same time felt a twinge on his neck. Almost automatically he reached for the area and began to scratch, digging his fingernails in deep to try to alleviate the pain.

He took his hand away and glanced down.

The tell-tale red and yellow indicated that he'd been successful in his efforts to burst the pimple.

He grunted with satisfaction and washed his hands and the teats of the cow before settling to his milking. Although he found the mechanics a chore he also enjoyed the time when he could wander off in to his thoughts and daydream.

Keith had been at school for three hours and had enjoyed the lessons so far. Mathematics 10 was a favourite as he cruised through the problems that were presented.

Science 10 was also interesting as he learnt so many new things every lesson.

He had just finished Physical Education and they had been learning new moves in gymnastics so he was sweating profusely.

His best mate, Bob Thompson was looking at him peculiarly and asked, "Are you alright KW?" Everyone called him KW or Lieutenant when he was at school.

"Sure, why do you ask?"

"You look like you've seen a ghost you are so pale. It's most unlike you," said Bob.

"Could be this damn pimple it's been annoying me for two days now. I wish it would go away," said Keith.

By home time Keith was feeling queasy and had difficulty mounting his horse.

No one saw him ride off but his father Fritz did see him riding in to the farm. Keith was hunched over and the horse was barely walking.

Fritz rushed out of the house and grabbed the reins of the horse saying, "Whatever is the matter son, you look terrible?"

"I don't know. I feel weak and hot," said Keith.

Fritz called to Phoebe who came running out to help Keith dismount and between them they carried him inside.

"I'll go for the doctor," said Fritz mounting Keith's horse. He spurred away.

Chapter 11

Ginger was standing under the apple tree leaning on a rake. He had the job of clearing up all the leaves and burning them.

It was autumn in the year 1924 and he was thirteen years old.

The leaves had been accumulating and the heap he had formed would fire up in a few minutes time.

Mr Chambers, the garden overseer, was on the war path so everyone was working slave like to try to avoid the cane that the grumpy old supervisor loved to wield.

George saw him approaching and began to furiously rake at the leaves. He scattered the heap to make it look like he had a lot more to do.

"Wit-taken, get here now," he yelled at George. The wit name had only begun a few weeks ago when one of the other supervisors was playing with words and names. He chanced upon the double take of George's surname and it had become a name of great jocularity.

"Coming sir, straight away," said George.

George's imagination ran wild and he braced for the stinging whack across his buttocks.

He approached to within a yard but nothing happened.

It had to be his lucky day but then what did the old bloke want?

"Go and get dressed in your finest my boy we have a sponsor who wants a look. Bring out your best manners and remember to lie to your teeth. If you're still here after he leaves then expect a visit from me," warned Mr Chambers.

As George went to run he caught a cuff under his ears and by the time he got to his bed the ringing was still there.

"A sponsor at last," he thought. "This has got to be my big break I don't want to stay here any longer."

He combed his hair, cleaned his teeth with the bicarbonate paste and ran to the office.

George sat bolt upright in a chair listening to the Orphanage manager waffle on about how brilliant the Orphanage was at turning wayward boys into fine young lads. "Loyal to a fault, hardworking, honest, well educated, well mannered..." the droning went on.

The potential sponsor finally spoke, "I'm looking for a strong lad to help me out on the farm. He needs to be able to milk the cows, plough the fields, that sort of thing."

George was awaken from his daydreaming and waited expectantly to be able to speak. The manager smiled showing his rotting teeth and said, "This here is the lad you need Mr Frisworth, that's exactly what he can do isn't it son?"

George was relieved to finally get a chance to speak. "Yes sir, I can milk and plough real good. And I can do anything you ask me to do."

Mr Frisworth's face showed a wry smile as he listened.

He was old and a little dottery but he was no man's fool.

He knew all about how these orphanages worked.

They belted the boys into submission, starved them to almost death and sold them off to the highest bidder.

"Son, you can go back outside now while I speak to Mr Frisworth," said the manager.

George got up and walked to the door. He hesitated and turned back, "Please take me sir and you won't regret it as I'm the best one left."

He went out and closed the door.

His future was now in the hands of an ailing, old farmer from Caterham. He could only sit and hope and wait.

Chapter 12

Keith was propped up in bed and Phoebe was fussing around him when the doctor from the Tweed Cottage Hospital arrived.

Phoebe didn't recognise him and he was quite young.

She knew most of the hospital staff as the whole family took delight in raising funds for the hospital.

Fritz had been the treasurer of the Hospital Auxiliary on many occasions.

"Now let me see what we have here," said the doctor placing his black bag on the end of the bed. On one side of the bag was Dr Abernethy written in large white lettering.

He checked Keith's temperature and 'tut tutted', checked his heart beat, checked up and down his arms and asked, "Have you any pain?"

Keith struggled to reply but indicated the back of his neck.

His throat was dry and felt swollen. He was having trouble swallowing and breathing.

The doctor looked at the redness and swelling around the pimple that Keith had scratched and a grave look came over his face. "I want the boy transported to the hospital immediately," he said.

Keith lay in the hospital bed wheezing and calling in agony.

Ever since the nurses had tucked him in the pristine white sheets he had been in agony.

The three hospital doctors had come and examined and left. They had sat in conference and discussed Keith's case. Each in turn had outlined the symptoms, their diagnosis and their conclusions.

It was now up to the head doctor to speak with the parents.

Fritz and Phoebe sat still in the foyer, holding hands.

They had been that way for nearly six hours.

The head doctor approached and they both stood up.

"Mr and Mrs Johnson," he began, "the news is not pleasant but it is my job to explain your son's case as best I can."

Phoebe burst into tears fearing the news would be grave.

"Your son has scratched a pimple on his neck and it has become infected. He has transferred a bug that is poisoning his entire system and I'm afraid that we have nothing that will stop it. He will be in utter agony while the poison flows throughout his body. It will then cause all the main organs to shut down resulting in his untimely death."

The doctor could see that his explanation was creating too much anxiety and he thought to stop.

However, he ploughed on, "I'm sorry but all we can do is sedate him so that he feels nothing in the way of pain. The process to death, unfortunately will take at least four days."

Fritz was holding his trembling wife and stoically listening to the doctor. He heard the word death and he shut down.

The doctor caught him as he collapsed and managed to carefully assist him to the ground.

Burton was away in the forest timber cutting and was unaware of the tragic situation that was unfolding at Murwillumbah.

Marion had been informed about Keith's hospitalisation and the diagnosis and she had sent out her brother Frank to try to locate Burton.

Unfortunately Frank had been given a wrong direction so it took him three days to find his brother-in-law

Burton immediately set off to the hospital.

When he arrived Keith had died and all he could do was weep for the wonderful young brother he had grown up with.

He rode out to the farm at Dunbible to console his mother and father.

His reception was not what he was expecting. His father turned on him in fury, "Where have you been while your brother suffered that agonising death? You didn't care as usual. Get out I never want to see your face in this house ever again. I no longer have any sons."

Burton wanted to explain and to tell his father he did care and that he was suffering Keith's loss as much as they were but he couldn't upset his father anymore.

He mounted his horse and rode away, not looking back at any time. He was parentless, an orphan forever.

As he rode along at a leisurely pace he felt his mind wandering and at times playing tricks on him.

At one point he saw a young lad approaching and was sure it was Keith. He even called to him but the youth just laughed and walked on.

He kept seeing strange movements to the left in his vision. He recalled someone mentioning the left field to him.

They had said, "Watch out for things that come from the left field". They had explained that things from left field are those you never expect.

Keith's sudden death was certainly from left field. Jack's terrible accident was one as well. He hoped that these left field things would go away and never revisit.

Keith William Johnson was buried at Murwillumbah in a ceremony that would be etched into the memory of those in the town for ever.

He was a truly popular young lad. At school he had excelled in athletics and was captain of the Murwillumbah School Athletics. He was a champion runner over 400 and 800 yards. He was an under officer in the school cadets and a scholar with the World at his feet.

Keith's passing was so sudden and so unexpected that people could not come to terms with it.

"How can a healthy young man who was saying hello one day be dead the next?"

The funeral was massive.

It began at the Hospital where Keith's casket was placed on a gun carriage pulled by four black horses.

Behind this was a small contingent of six soldiers from the Light Horse Battalion.

These were followed by the school cadets formed in threes.

The family and friends walked behind then the rest of the community.

The streets of Murwillumbah were lined by hundreds of onlookers.

This was the first ever Military Funeral to be held here and it was unique in that it was for an 18 year old cadet.

The procession took over an hour to wind its way down the steep hill from the hospital, along Wollumbin Street, up the hill passed the churches to the cemetery.

There was a graveside service given by the minister from the Church of England. During the service the Light Horse Brigade soldiers fired an 18 gun salute.

As each of the six blanks exploded the sound echoed

and reverberated across the hills and the Tweed valley. The sharp reload as the bolts were pulled back and then slammed into place made the graveside members flinch.

Bang, click, bang, click, bang.

Silence.

Then sobbing.

A mother had lost her youngest son at the age of 18.

Burton, Marion and many of the Stewart family attended the funeral but stayed well away from Phoebe, Fritz and Ruby.

Chapter 13

George was chewing on the sleeve of his shirt near his wrist when Mr Frisworth and the manager emerged from the office.

"Twenty days seems fine by me but I'm sure you'll find everything as ordered," said the manager.

"Come boy," said Mr Frisworth without even looking at George.

Eagerly George picked up the little case he had been made to pack and trotted off behind the old man.

Once outside George turned and looked back at the huge red brick walls of the institution that had been his home almost from birth. He hoped that he would never have to return.

"Come on son, keep up," said Mr Frisworth.

George's new home was a 40 acre farm on the outskirts of Caterham. The house was made of wood and it had a thatched roof. The front had a path leading from the road to the blue painted front door. A pretty garden with foxgloves and roses was pleasurable to the eye.

George watched Mr Frisworth search for and find the key from under the door mat.

He followed the old man into a neat lounge room,

down a corridor to a kitchen and then out another door to a bedroom.

"This is where you can bunk down George," said Mr Frisworth. "Mind you keep it neat and the bed made every morning. Now get comfortable while I put on the kettle."

George placed his meagre belongings into the drawer of a dresser and looked at himself in the mirror.

His shock of red hair made him laugh as it had been blown all over his head with the wind.

He made his way to the kitchen where Mr Frisworth was stirring his tea in a large brown mug.

Nearby was smaller, delicate china cup with flowers painted on the side, "One or two teaspoons of sugar?" he asked George.

"What's that?" asked George.

"You poor little bugger, they never let you taste sugar in there did they?" said Mr Frisworth. "Here taste this."

Mr Frisworth proffered a teaspoon to George who could see tiny little white crystals heaped on it. "This is sugar and it's used to sweeten things. Here taste it."

George obediently opened his mouth and swallowed. He immediately pulled a face and started coughing. "I can't stand that. Yuk."

"Well we'll leave that out of your diet. Feeding you will be simple fare and cost me less. Here drink up and I'll show you around the farm and point out your chores," said Mr Frisworth.

The farm was out the back and here there was a barn and a stall for milking. At the back boundary some 200 yards from the house was a canal that was used irregularly by barges carrying coal to and fro.

Ten cows, a horse, five pigs and a dozen chooks made up the menagerie.

There were several fruit trees and a small vegetable garden that looked overgrown with weeds.

"Now your jobs are to milk the cows once a day, separate the cream and the skim milk. The cream you take to the hotel where they will make it into butter to feed their customers. The skim milk you halve for the pigs and the kitchen. We can boil it and use it in our cooking and cups of tea. You let the chooks out to forage, collect their eggs and lock them away at night so the foxes don't kill them. The horse wanders with the cattle but in Spring you will use her to plough one of the paddocks and plant oats. The vegetable garden will need weeding and planting out. Some potatoes, spinach, carrots and turnips would be nice. Oh, and finally the front garden will need some care. Do you have any questions?"

George knew better than to ask anything so he said, "No sir I'll start right away."

Mr Frisworth spied from inside the house and chuckled to himself as he watched the wide eyed, eager young lad with the flaming red hair try to carry out the chores he had set him.

He knew full well that the lad didn't have the knowledge nor the skills to be a farmer.

He was more interested in the child's work ethic and his problem solving ability.

Although he got a laugh out of George's puny efforts to round up the horse he noted with admiration that he never gave up.

He was also impressed by the different ways he tried to catch the reluctant animal.

Finally Mr Frisworth wandered down to the far end of the property where George had corralled the horse and called out, "How's it all going, George?"

An exhausted George looked up and replied, "Fine Mr Frisworth I've nearly caught the horse. Then I'll harness him into the grader and cut out some of the weeds in the vegetable patch."

Mr Frisworth walked up to the horse and put his arms around it and used soothing words to calm it.

The horse stood still and then Mr Frisworth called George to come nearer and pat the horse's forehead. The change in the horse's behaviour was immediate and before long it was trusting of George.

"Always get to know the animal you are working with my boy and once you have their trust you will be able to get them to do almost anything. Remember too that they are usually well trained to obey you just need to learn what to say and do to get them to obey you."

George put the halter on the horse and led it towards the barn where the two handled grader was leaning against the wall. Mr Frisworth held the horse while George saddled the horse and harnessed it to the grader.

He stood behind the horse and put his head down.

"Mr Frisworth please don't send me back to the orphanage. I promise I will learn to be a hardworking farmer but I really don't know anything about farming."

He began to sob and hot tears ran down his ruddy cheeks.

Mr Frisworth came over and put his arm on George's shoulder and said, "I won't be sending back my best worker but I will be teaching him all about farming. You'll see you'll be a fine farmer before the year is out."

Winter came with a snow storm that left the entire district covered in over two feet of snow.

George and Mr Frisworth were snug inside their cottage with plenty of firewood to last the entire year.

George had learnt how to wield an axe and how to use the tomahawk to slice the thin pieces of kindling used to start the fire.

He had also shown how willing he was to carry out any chore by taking the horse and slide to the common some two mile away to cut fallen timber for the wood heap.

Throughout the winter months the camaraderie between the two had grown and Mr Frisworth knew his choice of a companion could not have been better.

The lad was a natural.

He learnt fast, he worked hard and he was good company even though he'd had limited life experiences.

Spring arrived with the ice and snow turning to slush. There was a flush of new growth as the grasses and flowers caught the change in temperature. Birds chirped and flew in all directions, many carrying twigs, leaves and hair to build their nests.

George was happiest when he could get outside and work.

He liked to see what he'd achieved after a day's work and enjoyed the encouragement from Mr Frisworth.

The vegetable garden sprang to life and was now double in size.

Mr Frisworth had wondered aloud why George had doubled the size and was left in admiration when George had explained, "I thought that we could barter with the neighbours for things we might need. They all said that they would love to get nice fresh vegetables from us."

George had never developed fully the skills to milk the cows.

He had spent almost two hours at his first try and when Mr Frisworth went to the barn to see what was taking so long he discovered a very frustrated lad with a blemish of milk in his bucket. "She won't give me any milk," he'd said meekly.

Mr Frisworth had taken over to show George his technique and within minutes the bucket was brimming with milk.

He then showed George how to use the separator to divide the milk into cream and skimmed milk. Next he brought the second cow into the stall and taking George's hands had shown him how to get the milk to flow freely from the cow's teats.

"Now, nice and easy and with confidence let's see you do the milking," said Mr Frisworth.

George tried to calm his shaking hands as he pulled down and squeezed. A spray of warm, white milk hit the side of the bucket and dribbled to the bottom.

He let out a cry of triumph and set to work in earnest.

It took him much longer to complete all four teats and to fill the bucket to three quarters.

As Mr Frisworth said, "It will take more time but once the experience and the rhythm locks in you will be a gun milker."

George loved getting outdoors and doing the work that he knew had to be done. Sometimes he worked so hard that he had all the chores done by lunch time.

In the afternoon he would wander off exploring the surroundings outside the farm.

George loved to say hello to the neighbours and other people whom he met.

One day he had gone to the back of the property to take a look at the canal. He knew it was there and Mr Frisworth had told him what it was used for. Other than that he didn't really know much more.

The afternoon was heating up when George bounded over the back fence and stood on the banks of the canal.

There wasn't a soul in any direction and from the look of the overgrown banks very few people bothered to venture near the canal at this point.

George scrambled along the steep incline pushing away long grass and vines that had grown wild.

He wondered how deep the middle was and if there was a current flowing.

George wasn't going to venture in as he didn't know how to swim and he'd heard that drowning wasn't a pleasant way to die.

He'd managed to make his way some 50 yards from where he started when he tripped over something in the grass.

He scrapped away the grass and mud and discovered a wooden boat. It was about ten feet long and three feet across at the centre. Some of the timbers were smashed and rotting but his close inspection revealed a rowing boat that could be salvaged.

Mr Frisworth wasn't all that keen on the idea of George in a boat on the dirty, smelly canal when George had come racing back full of enthusiasm about floating the boat.

He gave the boy reason after reason why it was too hazardous.

George took it all in and then changed tack, "If I could do it up and sell it we could make some money.

Mr Frisworth was intrigued by this suggestion and added, "It would also give you skills in wood working. The thing here is that I can't help you get the boat to the shed that will be up to you. You can use the tools in the barn. There's enough there to do any building job."

The job of getting the boat out of the canal and into the shed proved to be tough but half way through George came up with a brilliant idea.

He had taken the hoe and dug the boat out of the grass and mud. Then he had physically lugged it inch by inch towards the farm's back fence.

This was cumbersome and time consuming so he went to Mr Frisworth and asked him to help. "All you need to do is get the horse to do some pulling and I'll do the rest," he said.

George found a long piece of wire that he tied to the front of the boat and wound it out towards the back fence.

He threw it over and had Mr Frisworth back the horse up.

The wire was then tied to the slide.

George found a steel pole that was lying in the mud of the canal.

Mr Frisworth said it looked like something that had been on a barrage that floated up and down the canal.

The steel pole was hammered into the bank at the back fence with the wire around the side nearest the canal. With the horse giving pulling power and George guiding the boat they got it to the fence.

Here George up ended it and again with the horse pulling it was flipped over the fence. The rest was easy and before long the boat was upside down in the barn.

"You've got a lot of work there," said Mr Frisworth. "You make sure you don't neglect your other jobs."

George worked even harder on the farm and in the barn to get the boat shipshape.

He called on Mr Frisworth time and again to show him what the tools were for and how to use them.

He had to ask the best way to repair the boat and how to ensure it wouldn't leak once it hit the water.

Mr Frisworth proved to be very knowledgeable and it didn't surprise George, when one day, while they were caulking the boat's timbers with hot tar he confided, "This reminds me of the days in the navy on board the windjammers."

The boat was finished and sat on the grass outside the barn.

Two well-shaped oars lay in the bottom.

All George needed to do now was to get it in the water to see if it would float.

Mr Frisworth shot a warning to George, "You will not get in that boat on the canal until you can swim from one side to the other. I'll not have you drowning on my watch."

George knew better than to argue and besides learning to swim would add another arrow to his bow.

With Mr Frisworth and the horse assisting they reversed George's idea and soon had it floating in the canal. "Now my boy you need to come back up here while I try to teach you to swim, freestyle."

For five days George was taken to the back fence where he lay on the grass kicking his legs and moving his arms as if swimming.

Mr Frisworth was a hard task master but as he said, "If you don't get it right before you enter the water you'll sink like a stone and I won't be able to get you out. Caput, goodbye George.

He clicked his fingers and pouted.

George was rather coy in his first venture into the water and had to be urged along by Mr Frisworth.

He had a rope tied around his waist and the end was in Mr Frisworth's hands.

"It's freezing," he called as he inched his way in.

Once George had water to his waist Mr Frisworth said, "Duck under and wet your whole body. Now get ready to kick and use your arms like we've practised."

George set off but was a little slow to swing his arms and went under. He came up flailing about and choking.

He tried again and managed to do a few strokes but when he put his feet down to find the bottom it wasn't there.

George panicked and clawed the air with his fingers.

He sunk and came up again.

He took a breath of air and luckily heard Mr Frisworth calling, "Swim, swim like I taught you."

George lashed out for the shore and with Mr Frisworth pulling on the rope he got the momentum and soon reached shallow water.

"That's more like it. You were swimming as you came in, now try again," said Mr Frisworth.

George ended up being a strong swimmer and spent many summer hours swimming across the canal and back again.

He also learnt to launch the boat easily and to row it around the canal.

George was fast approaching his fourteenth year and was growing into a strong and handsome youth.

His knowledge and skills in farming were developing and Mr Frisworth wondered what he would do without him once he decided to go out on his own into the wide World.

George had no such thoughts in his mind.

George was happy working for Mr Frisworth and was accumulating a nice little bank as he saved the 20 pence he was given each week as his allowance. He was thrilled to receive a bonus every now and again and these added to his wealth. He never had a penny to his name when he left the orphanage.

One gloomy winter's night George and Mr Frisworth were sitting as close to the kitchen fire as they could without getting scorched when Mr Frisworth said, "Ever thought about your future my boy?"

The question frightened George and he hesitated.

"Obviously not," said Mr Frisworth. "Why I ask is because I'm not getting any younger and one day I will depart this earth and I won't leave you anything as it will all go to my son Peter. You should think about what lies ahead and where you might like to be in ten years' time."

George pulled the blanket he had around himself tighter to ward out the cold and thought about what Mr Frisworth was saying.

He was nearly 15 years old and had only ever been happy here with Mr Frisworth.

George knew what the old man was saying so he decided to contemplate long and hard about what he wanted out of life.

Things came to a head a few days later when George came back into the house after doing his early morning chores.

He rubbed his hands together and made a 'brrr' noise to indicate how cold he was feeling. The morning temperature was well below freezing and the ice covered ground was slippery.

George placed the five eggs he had found into the basin with the other dozen, put the freshly picked silver beet on the sink and sat down to rub his cold feet.

He stopped and listened but wasn't sure what it was he'd heard. He waited and then heard the distinct noise of a racking cough.

It was Mr Frisworth and George was alarmed at the noise he was hearing.

George sprung from his chair and walk into Mr Frisworth's bedroom. "Pardon my bursting in Mr Frisworth. You sound unwell and I need to ask if I can help you?"

Mr Frisworth lay in his bed, still and pale. He was so sickly that George thought that he was going to die.

The old man swallowed and said, "I've caught some horrible wog. My throat is sore and my chest is so choked up I can hardly breathe. Can you go to the apothecary and get me some medicine to alleviate my ailing?"

George was only too pleased to be able to assist as he could not bear to see his mentor in such a state of ill health. "What do you need, sir?" he asked.

"Explain to the apothecary my symptoms and ask if he can give you a tin of Richardson's Croup and

Pneumonia Salve and some mixture to stop the coughing," said Mr Frisworth.

He tried to lean over and reach out but the effort was too much and he slumped back on his pillow. "In the drawer, there's money," he rasped.

George walked around to the drawer and opened it.

He could see several one pound notes rolled into a bundle and tied with a piece of string. He untied the knot and took one of the notes before rolling the others up and tying up the string. He returned the money to its original place.

He tiptoed to the door, gathering his long coat and beanie.

Chapter 14

The walk to the shop was difficult as it was snowing and slippery with a fierce wind blowing directly into his face.

The shopkeeper greeted him, "Welcome my boy," he said. "What can we get for you today?"

The shop had a long wooden counter with glass in the lower part where a smorgasbord of goodies was arranged for all to see.

At the back of the counter were shelves packed with an assortment of herbs, spices and strange pieces of animals.

The apothecary was standing behind the counter in a white laboratory coat. He wore thick lensed glasses and had a serious look about him.

"Please, sir," said George, "I am the servant of Mr Frisworth and he ails with a sore throat, congested chest and difficulty of breath. He has sent me to ask you for a tin of Richardson's Croup and Pneumonia Salve. He would also like something for his persistent cough."

The apothecary disappeared out the back and returned with a small, brown tin with white writing all over it.

He handed this to George and said, "Read the

instructions so that you know what to do and I'll make up a cough mixture for Mr Frisworth. It will take me ten minutes."

George mumbled a thank you and started to read the writing on the tin. "Richardson's Croup and Pneumonia Salve made with a vaseline base with added camphor, nutmeg, eucalyptus oil and menthol. Rub a fingertip of ointment over chest and throat. Keep area warm. Continue treatment until cough and tightness of chest subsides. Rub it on, sniff it in, it's good for you. It's made by Presbyterians."

A few minutes the apothecary returned with a bottle of brownish liquid.

"It smells bad and tastes bitter but it will do the job. Mr Frisworth should take a teaspoon at night and again in the morning."

George thanked the chemist and handed over the pound note.

He received his change and then hurried outside.

The trip home was easier with a tail wind behind.

It reminded him of the Irish supervisor in the orphanage, who was always going around saying,

"May the road rise up to meet you.
May the wind always be at your back.
May the sun shine warm upon your face,
And rain fall soft upon your fields…"

Mr Frisworth was struggling to drink the medicine and George rubbed the ointment into his chest and around his neck.

He laid a folded towel across Mr Frisworth's chest before buttoning up his pyjamas top and covering him with the blankets.

For three days and nights George maintained a vigil over the ailing man.

He made him chicken broth and spoon fed him as much as he could swallow.

He emptied the bed pan and changed the towel on his chest while rubbing in the ointment and spooning out the cough mixture.

Mr Frisworth started to make progress towards a recovery but the ordeal had taken its toll on George.

He had too many hours to worry and too many to ponder his future.

He realised that one of them would have to leave one day and when that came the other would be lost. He decided it would be he who would leave.

But where was he going and how would he get there he dared not think too long about.

Mr Frisworth had run out of the rub and ointment and was still not back to his cheerful self so he sent George back to get some more.

The apothecary was pleased to hear that Mr Frisworth was recovering and immediately set about filling George's order.

As he waited George caught sight of a newspaper that was open on the counter. From his position it was upside down so he guessed the apothecary had been reading it.

He slowly turned it around and began to read the larger lettering of the headlines.

Nothing spectacular stood out until he got to the bottom right hand corner. Here he spotted an advertisement which had the title in uppercase lettering,

'COME FARM IN SUNNY QUEENSLAND'

George's heart skipped a beat and he picked the paper up and started to read the rest of the article.

He failed to hear the return of the apothecary and jumped with fright when a voice said, "Would you like to buy the paper as well?"

George realised he had been rather forward in reading the paper and thought he needed to apologise for his behaviour.

However, he said, "Do you know where Queensland is?"

The learned man behind the counter looked down at what George was pointing at and read out loud, "Come farm in sunny Queensland. The Australian Agricultural Group is offering special passage to farmers and farmers' labourers to sunny Queensland a state of the continent of Australia. Those wishing to apply can do so through their office at White Chapel Road in London. This is one chance in a life time to farm where the skies are always blue, the weather always fine and the sheep and cattle grow fatter. Well son that tells me you have a 12 thousand mile journey by ship to the Great South Land we all call Australia."

He paid a penny for the paper out of his own money and slipped it under his arm.

George paid for the medicines and paper and left the shop.

He was whistling loudly as he walked through the doorway of Mr Frisworth's house.

"Sounds like a fairy godmother has struck you with happiness my boy," said Mr Frisworth.

"I know where I want to go and what I want to do with my life," said George and he handed the paper to his mentor and friend.

"Australia. Well I never. I think you could be ready for this adventure but there is one problem we have to overcome. You see one of the rules when you were released to me from the orphanage was that you must stay indentured until you turn 15. The way I reckon the dates you still have some months to go."

George looked at Mr Frisworth and thought for a while.

A smile started to fill his face and he said, "When's my birthday?"

The old man scratched his chin and said, "To tell you the truth I was never told. The less you know the better for both of you was what the manager had said. Why do you ask?"

"Well you know I'm fourteen and that my next birthday will be my fifteenth so if my birthday was soon in the new year then that would make me 15 and I could leave legally."

"My gosh you're right so when do you want your birthday to be?" asked Mr Frisworth.

"Fifth of January, that sounds like a good date."
And so George was able to take his leave of the kindly Mr Frisworth on the 5th January 1926. The old gentleman gave him a hug and then stood back and offered him his hand. They shook hands warmly and wished each other all the best.

Then Mr Frisworth took a brown envelope from his shirt pocket and said, "This is a little something for all your kindness and hard work over the past three years. Use it wisely and if you ever come back this way you will always have a warm bed to sleep in and an ear to listen to all your wonderful adventures. Go with my blessing."

George strode out into the icy breeze making for the railway station that was some five miles north.

As he moved along he rehearsed the places he had to visit before he could finally clamber on board the ship that would take him to his new life.

He looked at the passing scenery and after a while noted a huge mansion to his right. It was set well back from the road that would take George passed the main gate. The grounds covered well over a hundred acres by George's estimation and he could see several figures working in various parts.

"This is a place fit for a king," thought George and wondered if his future would let him buy something similar.

The only way he could imagine owning something as majestic as this would be to be the heir.

Well an orphan like him had Buckley's chance.

George had to pass by the main wrought iron gates on his way to London and hopefully a ship to the Great South Land.

He had almost reached the entry when he noticed a rider on a white stallion riding out from the house.

He appeared to be in a hurry as the beautiful horse was galloping at speed.

By his estimation, George was of the opinion that this rider and he would run into each other just outside the gate.

He thought about stopping but something pushed him on.

The rider reined in hard and cursed, "What the hell you playing at boy. Get out of my damn road before I take a whip to you!"

"Sorry sir," said George and he lifted his head and looked directly at the tall gentlemen and saw his flaming red hair and piercing blue eyes.

He shuddered and thought for a fleeting moment that he'd looked into a mirror twenty years hence.

He jumped off the road as the rider spurred away.

Chapter 15

∞o∞

Marion looked down at her bulging stomach and felt the strong kick.

The second one was going to be a boy she was sure of that.

She edged closer to Burton and placed an arm around his broad shoulders.

She nuzzled into his neck and whispered, "I think it's time darling. The babe is starting to get restless."

Burton bounded out of the comfortable chair and began fussing around.

Marion stopped him and said, "I've got everything packed all you need do is call Frank to harness the horse to the gig."

The trip into Murwillumbah was free of incident but Burton kept being haunted by the thoughts of his brother's untimely death.

He hoped that nothing would happen to Marion or the baby as he'd had enough to contend with of late.

The staff of the Tweed Cottage Hospital was their usual helpful selves and efficiently transferred Marion into a bed.

They ushered Burton out and told him to stop worrying

as they would take good care of mother and child.

Burton Mackie Johnson came quickly into the World on 17th July 1914.

His arrival was met with much jubilation at the Stewart farm.

The celebrations may have continued for weeks as Burton was so excited about producing an heir he couldn't help himself.

Unfortunately the World events put paid to the family happiness when on 28th July it was announced that Great Britain was at war. This meant Australia and all the dominions would be expected to recruit fighting men to help the King.

Marion arrived home with her new son a week later and to her dismay discovered that all the talk around the table was about the war.

Worse still the conversation led to her brothers talking about signing up.

Reuben had said, "This shouldn't take long so if we're going we need to sign up immediately. By the time we sail to Europe the whole nonsense will be over. At least we get a holiday, see the sights of Europe and get paid. It sounds too good to me."

The next morning Marion was shocked to find Reuben and Don dressed in their best suits and saddling their horses. She said, "I think you are wrong Reuben. Any war is horrible and only bad can become of it. Please I beg you not to take Don. He's not yet 18 and he's only a child at heart."

"He's big enough to make up his own mind, sis, I'm only offering to be his companion."

As they rode off Marion's twin brother, Hersee tapped her on the shoulder and said, "I'm going too and so is Jack."

"Hasn't Jack been through enough already? They won't take him with that silver plate in his head," said Marion.

"I think they will," said Hersee. "He wants to help out by joining the Field Ambulance Corps."

All four were taken into the Australian Infantry Forces and sent off to the various training grounds.

Don had been selected after he put his age up declaring he was 18 and 4 months.

Marion and Mary Jane wept their hearts out when the four boys came home, dressed in their smart khaki uniforms on furlough.

They proudly showed off their slouch hats and the shiny rising sun badge on the side.

They took their Lee Enfield 303s and marched around the farm to show off their training drills.

"Have they trained you in real war like conditions such as hand to hand fighting?" asked William John.

"Of course they have," said Reuben, "And bayonet training."

"Seems to me that you really don't know what you are all in for. War is very ugly and casualties can suffer for the rest of their lives," said William John.

"Or be killed," said Marion somewhat prophetically.

The four soldiers were all too keen to have their fun and then go overseas and deal with the Germans and Turks to listen to any of the advice.

They finished their leave, packed up and left to fight overseas.

Three of the men would return alive but Rueben paid with his life. He was killed at Pozieres on 23rd July, 1916.

While everyone was still in mourning for Rueben, Marion gave birth to her second daughter, Evangeline. She came bawling into the World on the fourth of August 1916. The little one would be forever called Eva.

As the war came to a faltering conclusion Marion produced her third daughter she named Isobel. She was born on the 26th June 1918.

Burton was immensely proud of his growing brood and of his wonderful wife.

He had been busy farm labouring and keeping his head down as he definitely thought going away to fight in a war was futile.

Mary Jane was slowly turning against him as she saw the sacrifices of her sons while he remained a pacifist.

She had taunted him one day by saying, "Even Jack, bless his soul, was willing to give something to the cause by going in the medical corps. He didn't have to fight, but you, Burton won't even contemplate helping."

Burton's days were spent learning as much as he could about farming and the skills he needed to be successful.

In early 1923 he went to speak to his father-in-law, William John Stewart about share farming.

It wasn't about share farming with William John because he had already semi-retired and was living on the farm. He had offered the farm to his son George who had accepted.

The war, death of Rueben, the accidental shooting in the buttocks of Don by friendly fire, the gassing of his sons and old age had slowly taken their toll.

William John and Mary Jane stayed in the homestead and Burton and his family were there too.

The family had grown one more when Keith was born just after Christmas on the 30th December, 1923.

Burton was so excited to have a second son because it allowed him to fulfil a promise he had made to his brother Keith way back at the funeral of his brother.

Standing in the crowd but feeling alone he had looked to the heavens and said to himself, "One day I will have a son and I will call him Keith William after you. I solemnly promise you."

Burton had been made an offer to share farm with

Charles Bignell a well to do farmer who preferred city life to the sticks.

He had a sixty acre holding on the Pumpenbil Road and was looking for someone to share farm with

William John explained how things worked in that usually one supplied the land and animals and the other the labour and know how.

Generally it worked out with profits split as per the contract. Most land owners expected more of the profits than the worker.

William John did caution Burton about going in too deep and being too trusting.

He concluded by suggesting that he make sure he had a watertight contract signed before proceeding.

Burton mulled this over but didn't quite get to the point where he approached anyone to become a share farmer with.

Unfortunately William John began to ail during the year of 1923 and passed away in Tyalgum 5th January, 1924.

Burton had lost his mentor so he was now on his own. Whatever decision he made was on his head and his alone.

After consideration Burton determined that working for himself was a better prospect than working for others.

He could use his ingenuity to increase productivity which would then lead to him being an owner in his own right.

He went to see Charles Bignell only to discover that he had already set up a leasing with another.

Disappointed, but not ready to give up, Burton asked around and finally found another possibility.

Alf Gibson was ailing from war wounds and could no longer work his farm 6 mile from Tyalgum on the Murwillumbah Road. He offered Burton the share farming on condition that it was done quietly and on a hand shake.

Burton agreed forgetting the sound advice William John had offered before his demise.

Burton was convinced to pay his first year up front and that resulted in his clearing his entire bank account.

He wasn't worried as he found Gibson a likeable chap and the farm had potential in capital letters and flashing lights.

By the end of the second year Burton estimated he would have made his investment three times over and be set to buy his own freehold farm.

He set to work and within three months had the farm working like a well-oiled machine. He was milking 40 head of cows, running pigs, poultry and had ploughed and planted 30 acres of crop.

The crop alone would fetch a good price and he would need less than a quarter as feed for his animals.

Burton couldn't believe how well he was doing.

He should have foreseen that when things were too good to be true then they probably were.

Watch out for the left field should have been his ingrained motto.

Chapter 16

The noise at the bar was louder than he could stand but he didn't move but stared vacantly across the table he was sitting at. How he got here he couldn't recall.

The last thing he remembered was the sharp bang of the judge's gavel as it hit the wooden desk.

As his mind began to clear and reality returned he was shocked to discover he was in one of God's forbidden establishments.

He peered at the little glass that laid half empty in front of him and pondered what evil spirit he had ordered and what that was doing to the pure blood that was pulsating through his veins.

Marion would be aghast if she saw him in a hotel and would invoke it as the Devil's work.

The noise was still coming from the bar where three young blokes and an older man were drinking golden liquid from rather large glasses. He surmised that it was beer but he really had no knowledge of this side of life.

He heard the old codger, thick set, dark curly hair and dressed in dirty overalls enquire of the bartender, "What the hell is the God-fearing Burton Johnson doing in here, and drinking firewater?"

The man behind the bar made a shushing sound

and replied, "Leave it alone Curly I think he's had a bit of bad news. He's drinking water with a touch of lemon juice, I might add, and trying to pluck up courage to go home and tell the missus that their World is about to implode."

Curly was not to be swayed from his mission.

Here was a chance to take one of those sanctimonious Stewart-Johnson clan down a peg or two.

All too often he had heard them preaching in the street or had his little woman return from their makeshift church out on their selection at Bray's Creek and tell him he was a sinner.

He'd kept his mouth shut for peace and so that he could still get under the sheets with her and have his way. Upset her and she would go from cuddly, sweet and compliant to cold, remote and huffy. The latter could last for days and for a man who worked away a lot it meant missing out on the greatest pleasure of all especially as it was Betsy offering it.

"Hey Johno or should I call you 'Chicken Little', what's the problem? Come over here and have a beer with us."

The three hanger-ons chuckled and pushed each other as they saw a confrontation about to happen.

A good old fashioned fist fight was in the making.

Burton didn't say anything.

He seemed to have receded back into himself again. He was deeply troubled and didn't need any more things to contend with.

The bartender picked up the piece of four by two that he kept behind the counter and rested it on the counter a yard away from Curly. "I want no trouble in here Curly and Burton isn't looking for any either so let's leave it be."

Curly wasn't to be deterred and went on to a bullying tact. "Hey Chicken Little the sky fall in did it? Didn't feel anything over here. Did youse boys hear that the sky had fallin' in?"

"No sirree," chorused the band of agitators.

"Right, that's it!" shouted the bartender slamming the hunk of timber on to the bar.

The noise was ear splitting and the three younger ones stepped back from the bar and turned to leave.

"You've got thirty seconds to drink up and get out before I blow my whistle and start tapping ankles," warned the barman.

Curly grabbed his beer raised it and said, "Cheers sir," then turned towards Burton and continued, "Cheers Chicken Bertie for now but I'll be waiting somewhere some dark night for you. This hasn't been finished."

With that as a salute he downed the more than half a glass of amber liquid in one gulp.

He thumped the schooner on the counter and charged out.

The three stragglers rushed to catch up, slamming the door as they went.

A few seconds later the sound of hooves and a "Heeya" split the silence.

"Thank gawd they're gone and good riddance to them. These fly by nighters are all too prevalent around here at the moment," said the barman.

From the back corner a tiny squeaky voice asked, "Where's here?"

"Oh my gosh!" said the barman, "You really are in a bad way Burton. Let me rustle up someone to help you home to that lovely little lady and kids of yours. By the way, the here, is Tyalgum and you are sitting in the hotel in the main street. Does that help?"

The bartender walked out the back and returned a few minutes later with a young stripling about 15 years old. He was wearing grey shorts held up by black braces. He had a green shirt on that was wet across the shoulders and here layers of dust had formed a muddy smear.

"Lyle, my boy's been loading the kegs into the cellar but he has agreed to take you out to your selection. Come on we'll get you home."

The two good Samaritans walked over to the table and the barman offered his thick brawny hand to Burton. Like a meek lamb Burton gripped the hand and used its strength to lever himself from the chair.

He then let Lyle put his arm around his shoulders and together they teetered towards the door.

Once outside they could see Burton's roan standing patiently for his master.

They helped him mount and Lyle took the reins and set off at a trot leading horse and rider down the main street.

In the background they could see the ominous peak of Mount Warning. It was the core of an extinct super volcano that had erupted millions of years ago.

All around were mountains some near and some far away all blanketed by thick forest.

The lower slopes had been cleared by the timber cutters some 50 years ago. These hardy men were the true pioneers of the area.

They pushed inland in search of the red cedar that fetched a king's ransom but it took muscle and loneliness to win and many times even life.

All the red cedar was now gone and in its place the rich volcanic soil was lush with grasses and farmers were making commercial use of this.

As they trotted along Burton seemed to be oblivious to his surroundings.

Lyle on the other hand was enjoying the crisp, fresh air and was taking in the environs that he was passing through.

It added to his cheeriness that he had escaped the hotel cellar and the dirty back breaking job of lifting heavy beer kegs off the dray and man handling them into the cellar down those steep steps.

He was especially happy because he had a five nice

shiny 2/- pieces in his left hand. The bribe his father had used to get him to escort Mr Johnson home.

He had plenty of ideas of what he could spend this money on including saving some for later so he could buy a dairy farm and make butter like lots of the others in the Tyalgum and Bray Creek area.

He knew that Mr Johnson was a dairy farmer and it must have paid well as he was always well dressed and he rode a beautiful roan.

Not only that but he had five kids and his wife drove around the district in a horse and buggy.

She was also a keen churchgoer and Lyle's mum often went out to the Johnson house for church.

He never did because his dad reckoned it was a lot of nonsense praying to someone you couldn't see and what with all the evil and death in the World shouldn't this God be looking after us and keeping us safe?

Still deep in thought Lyle turned the bend in Coolaman Street headed past the Butter Factory until he reached the junction at Coodjie Street.

Here he took a right turn past the Tyalgum Road then continued on into Bray's Creek Road.

He slowed to a walk. The gradient was quite steep ahead and he needed to conserve some energy for the four miles that lay ahead.

The bush on either side was thick as it was a remnant of the original forest.

From a bend at the top of the hill he could look out

across the Bray Creek Valley. Most of this had been cleared by the tree fellers and the incoming farmers who followed many years later cleaned up their selections and turned them into open space valuable farms.

In the Bray Creek Valley most of the selectors had turned to dairying.

As the numbers increased so did the need for a local Butter Factory.

This was finally realised and the whole Tyalgum farming community flourished.

Before the Tyalgum Butter Factory was built the farmers resorted to getting the cans of milk into the Flat where it was then taken the 19 miles to Murwillumbah. Some days the connection was not made for various reasons resulting in the milk conveyor to continue his ride all the way into the bigger town.

Lyle seemed to be enjoying his walk as he strode out along the track.

He knew all the farms and the families that inhabited each log building.

As he passed each he mentally went through the names of all the children in the family. Some were easy as they had only six, others bordered on the ridiculous as they had nurtured 15 children and many of these had already left for greener pastures.

At long last he topped the hill and below he could see the Stewart family home.

Johnson, the silent rider he was taking home was married to one of the daughters and ever since old man Stewart had died he had been living with his mother-in-law.

The house was very large for the Bray's Creek area.

It had originally consisted of one main room where sleeping was the main activity.

A lean-to was built for cooking and a verandah to relax on during hot days.

Over the years a new house had been built to accommodate the growing family.

One of the oddities of the place was that the old cabin had now been converted into a church. Here at all sorts of times and days people would arrive to pray, seek forgiveness or guidance.

Lyle noted that there was greyish smoke wending its way skywards from the each of the four chimneys.

The inside would be snug and warm as outside it was still quite crisp.

Lyle hastened his step into a trot and began to smile widely.

One of the real reasons he had not argued with his father when he was sent on this long and ardu-ous trip was that he had a yearning for one of the Stewart girls.

He was hoping against hope that she would be home, even come running out to thank him for his thoughtfulness and ask him in for a hot chocolate or even a cold drink would do.

Burton had not said a word all the way and even the lengthening of the horse's stride had not perturbed him.

He sat ramrod straight staring with unseen eyes ahead. He had not acknowledged Lyle at any time over the past hour that they had been on the road.

Lyle could see movement way ahead near the homestead and realised that someone had noticed his approach. Hopefully one of those people would be his secret love.

Mrs Stewart, most called her Mary Jane, was at the kitchen table wearing a white apron that stretched all the way below her knees. This was tied neatly around the waist with a white ribbon.

Beneath the apron she wore a white frock that covered her from neck to the ankles.

Her short greying hair was hidden under a bonnet.

It was baking day and she was in deep concentration kneading a large piece of dough. With each punch into the mass, clouds of flour rose and fell.

Next to her was her daughter Merion, although everyone called her Marion.

She was taller than her mother and always had a ready smile. She also wore the same outfit as Mary Jane.

Her hair was dark brown and although not long was held up with a green ribbon that was tied into a bow. The green of the ribbon matched her aquamarine eyes.

She grinned at her mother and said, "You'll have us all looking like ghosts if you keep that up mother. The flour clouds are getting in everyone's hair."

The everyone, referred to the Johnson daughters Madeline and Eva who were also standing around the table.

They each had dough in front of them and each was at a different stage in the making of scones.

They worked as a team in accomplishing the task quickly and efficiently.

Mary Jane was the bread maker and prided herself in turning out fresh loaves that would last the week for the whole family and visitors too.

The other members of the group were busy kneading dough, rolling dough out with a wooden rolling pin, cutting the circles of dough using a glass or brushing each with a brush dipped in cow's milk.

Once ready they would be placed on the huge trays and slipped into the two tiered oven and baked for 20 minutes.

The bread of course had to wait for the yeast to rise before it was shaped into a loaf and placed in the bread baking tray.

The frenetic activity was brought to a premature

halt with the sudden loud yelling of a young girl some-where outside. "Someone's coming. Mum it looks like daddy and he's got a boy with him."

Marion gasped and ran towards the door desperately trying to brush the dough and flour that was sticking to her hands and fingers. "Whatever could the matter be?"

Behind her she heard her mother's voice imploring, "Now Marion don't take the negative there's probably a reasonable explanation for this."

Outside the voice who had warned them all could be heard running away up the road calling, "Daddy, daddy you are home. I love you."

Lyle was now in easy sight of the house and could hear the yelling and the approaching little girl.

Out of the main door way came an adult all covered in white followed by an identical but more portly female.

As he prepared his speech he noted two more chil-dren come running out of the doorway and rushed passed the two adults.

The roan was spooked by all the calling and running and tossed its head away.

Luckily Lye had a firm grip and was able to quieten the horse.

Burton still had not moved.

By now the vanguard had arrived closely followed by the second wave. The two adults held back at the front gate of the home paddock.

"Hello daddy," called the first young girl. She was about five years old dressed in shorts and a blouse, all matching of white calico. She had ginger, wavy hair and a toothy smile. Her hair was in plaits that hung down to her waist.

The other girls arrived.

The oldest was eleven and the other eight. Each was almost identical to the five year old in hair colour.

All three were unmistakably sisters and the man on the horse was clearly their father.

His ginger curly locks matched theirs.

The eldest took charge and asked her father. "Why is this boy leading your horse dad?"

Lyle was quick to call out to the adults, "I need your help missus as Mr Johnson isn't feeling too good."

Marion ran forward and took hold of one of Burton's legs, "What's the matter darling?" she asked.

"No good talking to him missus he ain't spoken since we left the pub," offered Lyle.

"Not spoken, pub what are you talking about?" demanded Mary Jane who had also come forward to help.

"Will you talk some sense, boy? What are you up to Burton get off that horse and come inside."

She was used to being in charge so was somewhat taken aback when Burton stayed stock still and silent.

With Lyle's help and advice the two women managed to get Burton from the horse and into a standing position.

"Oh my poor love," whispered Marion, "What has afflicted you?"

Mary Jane turned to Lyle and dismissed him with, "Thank you boy for helping him home you'd better be getting back before the dark sets in."

With that she helped Marion with her ailing son-in-law through the gateway, along the path and through the front door.

They manhandled him into the spare bedroom where Marion and Burton had been staying and let him flop onto the double bed.

Marion fussed around making him comfortable, removing his riding boots, removing his tie and taking off his breeches and shirt. She tucked him in, kissed his forehead and closed the door.

All the while Mary Jane kept up a tirade, "He's been in the Devil's Pit and he's imbibed the Devil's own drink and he comes back here drunk. I told you this would happen one day."

"Shush, mama," said Marion, "We don't know what happened so let him rest and then we'll see what the story truly is. In the meantime I'll send Frank into town to find Dr Sommerville. Burton needs a thorough medical check. I can only ask that we all pray for our loved one to be alright."

Marion walked out of the bedroom and gently closed the door. She looked around the kitchen and saw a room full of young worried faces. All the children were sitting at the long table waiting patiently for a verdict as to what was wrong with their adored father.

Mary Jane continued fussing around the stove moving the large cauldrons that spluttered and bubbled. The stew and soup she had been cooking were likely to spoil now that there appeared to be a major family crisis at hand.

Chapter 17

Marion addressed the children in a confident voice although deep inside her heart was thumping with anxiety, "Your father has had a turn and we must do a number of things to help him and find out what afflicts him. Madeline and Eva as the older two I want you to run like the wind down over the creek to find Frank. He is pulling out the last of the stumps in the north paddock. Tell him I need him back here at all haste. Don't tell him what is wrong as that may cause him to make too much effort and result in an accident. Once he is away please come home quickly to help your grandma out."

The two girls stood up and chorused together, "Yes mum."

The taller of the two was Madeline and she had a serious demeanour, one full of responsibility that came with the job of being the eldest. Her brown hair had wisps of red through courtesy of her father. She wore a homemade dress of cotton, green with light spots of brown. The waist was tied with a ribbon of light blue. She wore dark brown long socks and black slip on shoes.

As she left the kitchen she reached out to a number

of hooks in the hallway and snatched a yellowy bonnet and once outside pulled it down over her head.

Her hazel eyes showed the signs of business and urgency as she turned to her younger sibling and urged, "Come on Evie let's race each other to the other side of the creek."

With that she kicked off her shoes leaving them on the path and took flight.

Eva, or Evangeline as she had been christened and the name that mum insisted everyone call her, didn't hesitate and also relieved herself of the shoes and took flight.

Eva was only a few inches shorter than Madeline but was thinner and took life as it came.

She wasn't borne down with the feeling of total responsibility but she did have a strong work ethic.

Her mother and grandma were her role models and ever since she could toddle she would be sat on one or the other's knees to help make dough, peel vegetables, wash the dishes and even milk the cows. Her bed was always neatly made and her clothes washed and ironed.

As she ran to catch up to the flying Madeline she pulled her cream bonnet down over her brownish-red wavy hair.

She had a determined look in her eyes as she pushed herself to the limit recalling the urgency in her mother's voice.

Her long white dress slowed her through the thick, lush grass that grew prolifically across the entire valley. That's what made the Bray's Creek so famous for its dairy cattle.

Eva was still about five yards behind Madeline as they reached the creek.

At this point it was quite shallow and was often used by the family as a ford.

On the side they were approaching from there was a sand bank about two yards wide then a pebble strewn gully over which water gurgled and bubbled.

The water was only a few inches deep.

The ford was altogether ten yards wide and at either end were deep pools.

On the far side of the creek was a steep embankment.

Madeline made short work of the sandbar and then splashed through the water before tackling the eroding embankment.

She scrambled up, almost reached the top, flung out a hand to grab a piece of creeper growing at the top, missed and came tumbling down again. She slid under the oncoming Eva who hadn't thought to stop or weave.

They crashed together at the bottom and ended up in the cold water together.

"Come on let's get a move on. Sorry sis but we can't stop now," shouted Madeline.

She jumped up, grabbed Isobel's outstretched hand and hauled her to her feet.

Together they tackled the embankment and scrambled over the top.

"Nothing hurt I hope?" asked Madeline.

"Nah," came the shaky reply even though Eva could make out a trickle of red starting to run down her left shin where she could make out a tear in her sock. "Let's push on and fast."

As they raced out of the thick rainforest that bordered the creek they could make out Uncle Frank and old Chaffy way in the distance and knew their target was in reach.

Frank was Marion's youngest brother and one of the few left at home to help with the farming chores.

He was approaching his eighteen birthday.

He had been sent to the bottom paddock by his mother, after milking, to clear the final three stumps that stuck out and caused a hazard during ploughing and harvesting. They were the remnants of a once proud rainforest that had clothed all the mountains, hills and valleys throughout the Tyalgum area.

He had been here with Chaffy, the huge grey draught horse since 5.00am and was in the final throes of extracting the last of the giant stumps.

He estimated that each had to have been three hundred year old red cedar trees.

These magnificent trees had once grown everywhere in the rainforests of Queensland. They had been cut down by the timber cutters who pioneered the wilderness and opened the way for the dairymen.

Chaffey stood patiently some two yards clear of where Frank toiled with an axe and a shovel.

He had to dig around the roots that wormed their way in every direction from the trunk. These gave the gigantic trees the stability to stay upright in all weather and on any incline.

The tap root fed and watered them and gripped the earth many yards underneath the soil.

The tap root was dug into on one side and a roaring fire set into it. This was always on the lee side so that the heat would be blown away from the worker who kept finding and cutting the roots on the windward side.

Once he snapped the outriding roots and knew that the fire had worked its way well into the tap root he was ready for Chaffy to pull the whole root out.

The other two stumps were not as big as this final one and they were sitting on their sides stacked together nearby.

Frank looked up from within the hole when he thought he heard voices from afar.

He could barely see over the hole he had dug and the fire from the other side was creating a shimmering affect to his vision.

He squinted again and searched the paddock out towards the creek. Sure enough he made out two people running like crazy as though chased by a bull.

His instincts told him something was amiss back at the homestead.

He clambered towards the horse and began frantically to unhook the chains that were attached to the saddle and ran down and around the log. These would be used by Chaffy to haul the log out of the hole and over to the other two nearby.

He took a flying leap onto Chaffy's back and the huge horse didn't move.

He had been trained well and had come to understand what his masters required of him.

A few kicks in the ribs and a call of, "Away boy," was enough for him to set off at a trot towards the advancing girls.

The distance between the horse and rider and the two girls diminished rapidly as Chaffy got up to a canter.

"What's the hell's going on?" called Frank as he came up to Madeline.

Out of breathe but determined to pass the message Madeline gasped, "No questions, grandma and mum need you urgently."

With that he kicked Chaffy a few more times and the huge horse responded and away they flew.

Chaffy's long black tail stuck straight out behind and Frank held tight to the long, hairy black mane.

"Go, go, go," urged the two girls.

Then Madeline added an afterthought, "And don't use blasphemous words, Uncle Frank Stewart!"

With that the girls flopped to the ground exhausted.

Frank and Chaffy took the ford at almost a gallop and tore across the home paddock.

The huge draughthorse came to a halt at the front gate and Frank slipped from his back and ran inside.

"What's going on?" he shouted as he entered the kitchen.

Marion explained what had happened and then added, "I want you to do the following things as a matter of urgency. The first is to hook Blankets to the gig, set out to Tyalgum and along the way you should run into young Thoms. Pick him up and thank him for looking after my Burton and give him this 2/- coin. After you drop him off at the hotel go to Doc Sommerville and bring him back here."

Frank took the shiny coin, slipped in his pants pocket and ran out the back door.

Halfway to the creek was the milking sheds and the barn.

He strode into the barn, grabbed the handles of the gig and pulled the cart out into the yard.

He whistled and called for Blankets who surprising cantered up to the railed fence and waited to be saddled. Frank took the saddle from the post where it always rested, opened the gate for the horse to walk through. He saddled the horse, tied the handles of the gig in place, climbed aboard and set off at a jaunty pace.

As he went passed the house Marion and his mother waved and he dipped his hat to them.

He loved being out and about with Blankets. She was his favourite horse. Her jet black coat and high stepping gait made her the envy of every other boy and farmer in Bray's Creek.

His father had bought her at a sale only a year and a half ago as a two year old.

He had patiently broken her in and taught her how to trot with a high step action.

Unfortunately his father didn't get to use her much as he had passed away.

They cantered past a number of selections as the sun slowly sunk over Mount Warning.

It was always a thrilling sight to see the sun setting over the chimney of such an ancient volcano. It gave off the reds, oranges, yellows and purples that changed every second and gave the look of an active volcano erupting.

Up ahead Frank caught a glimpse of someone walking on the road and hoped it was Lyle.

He thought the kid was okay even though they weren't really friends.

He wouldn't have been allowed to be seen with someone whose father sold the Devil's drink no matter how nice they were.

He slowed Blanket and called out, "Hey Lyle, jump aboard and I'll run you home."

"Much obliged," replied Lyle and ran alongside before putting one foot on the running board and clambering up on to the seat.

Frank gave Blanket a switch with the whip and she set off at a gallop.

"Marion sent me along to take you home. She also said to thank you for your help and kindness and as a reward she offers you a coin."

With that explanation Frank pulled out the coin and handed it to Lyle who took it, grinned and shoved it in his pocket. A faint jingle could be heard as the coin joined the other five.

Lyle had done well today and he was now being conveyed rapidly home so would be in time to fiddle the cat's whisker and listen to his favourite serial on the radio.

After dropping Lyle off at the Hotel and thanking him once again, Frank set off for Dr Sommerville's surgery.

Frank thought about the kindly old man with his balding head and grey locks. He had let the side hair grow to compensate for the loss on top which made him look like a mad professor when the wind blew.

Frank halted the horse in front of the hitching rail and after alighting, tied the reins.

He knocked on the front door and called out, "Doc, it's Frank Stewart, we need you urgently there's something amiss with Burton."

The urgency in Frank's voice wasn't lost on the doctor as he appeared within seconds, still pulling his grey overcoat on and carrying his bowler hat.

In the other hand he carried his doctor's bag with his name and qualifications neatly painted white on black.

"Let's away boy and you can fill me in as we go. It could be another long night but that's what a doctor's life is all about."

Frank untied the horse, climbed up on to the seat, turned the horse's head for home and set off.

They galloped along Coolaman Street and after turning right entered Bray's Creek Road.

"This was the same route taken by Lyle earlier today when he brought Burton home," thought Frank.

As they galloped along Frank began to tell the doctor what he knew of Burton's affliction and the goings on over the afternoon.

He wasn't all that aware of too much as he had been under urgent orders since finding the girls in the paddock.

Doc Sommerville sat quietly musing over the information he had gleaned from the lad, scratched at his chin and said, "Sounds like a mental breakdown or God forbid, a stroke."

Chapter 18

Marion peeped around the corner of the door and was pleased to see the shape of her husband breathing beneath the blankets.

It was early morning and the sun had yet to rise over the mountains to the east.

She tiptoed to the edge of the bed so she could get a better look at his face. The colour had returned and she heaved a quiet sigh.

The doctor had spent some time trying to get some sense out of Burton but without success.

He had resorted to shining a torch in one eye and then the other in quick flicking movements.

After a while his diagnosis was received by everyone who had crowded in the room, "He's had a nasty shock which has affected his memory and left him morose. A few days rest and lots of loving care and he'll be back on his feet as new."

Marion smiled to herself as she recalled the comments and felt the heavy burden lift from her shoulders.

"Marion is that you my darling?"

Burton was still laying ever so still but his voice was strong.

"Yes Burton, I came to see if you need anything as you haven't eaten for over 18 hours. Maybe some soup, a piece of damper with butter and a nice cup of black tea with sugar?"

"That would be nice, thanks."

With that Marion scurried from the room and went to prepare the food.

She was smiling widely as she walked into the kitchen that was off the side of the house.

Her mother, Mary Jane, was already there busily making toast for the other members of the family.

Marion announced as she bustled in, "He's talking and has asked for something to eat."

"That's lovely to hear," said Mary Jane. "The children will be pleased to hear that their father is feeling better. You will need to find out what has afflicted him, my dear, and why he was in that hotel."

She almost spat the final two words and a look of thunder came across her face.

Marion collected the damper, spread it with butter and poured a cup of black tea into an enamel mug. She spooned three teaspoons of sugar into the tea and gave it a brisk stir.

She set the food on a wooden tray and walked out the door heading for the bedroom.

She was pleasantly surprised but unhappy to see Burton was up and dressed in his work outfit.

He was tying the laces on his riding boots as she entered.

She put the tray on the bed and he hungrily began to eat the damper and gulp down the tea. It was clear to see that he was starving.

"Now my dear," Burton began, "I want you to gather everyone in the front room as need to talk to them all. That includes your mother and brothers."

Marion did not question the commands and set off to find everyone and summons them into the large front room that was used for lounging around after long hours of work.

Often the family would play games or have long discussions here.

It took barely ten minutes to find everyone who lived at the farm and get them assembled in the lounge room.

Burton was waiting patiently as the last of the stragglers entered and sat on the bare wooded floor in front of him.

Burton stood to attention and with a quiet voice said, "I need Marion to tell all of you what happened to me as I have little recollection. The last thing I can recall is going into the Murwillumbah Court House and the judge declaring me bankrupt before he banged the gavel on his desk."

He sagged into the comfortable chair behind him.

Marion was already on her feet and coughed as she was not expecting to say anything. She cleared her throat to gain time and compose herself.

She was a short but striking woman, round faced

and a prominent jaw. Her Scottish and English ancestry showed through her features.

She looked towards her husband and addressed him directly.

The other members of the room concentrated on what they were about to hear.

Each had a snippet of the story and all had bits missing.

"Yesterday you left early on your horse to ride into Murwillumbah to attend to some business. You didn't tell any of us why you were headed that way. I made you some damper, cheese and tea for your journey. At about 4 pm Lyle, the hotel keeper's son, brought you home on your horse. We all helped you into your bedroom. You were in a dreadful state and not talking."

At this point tears welled into Marion's aquamarine eyes and she choked out her words.

Stoically she stemmed the flow of tears and continued on. "Lyle was able to tell us that you had arrived in the hotel at 11.20am, sat at a table and wouldn't speak to anyone. You just stared into space. His father had given you a drink which at one stage you had sipped. His father then sent him to lead your horse home here. We sent Lyle on his way and then I got the girls to run to the bottom paddock to fetch Frank. Frank saddled up Blankets and put her in the gig. He drove into town, picking up Lyle on the way and paying him 2 shillings. He then sort out Dr Sommerfield and brought him at the gallop back here to attend to you. His diagnosis was that you had a serious fright that had created a shutdown of parts of your memory resulting in amnesia. He said it was unlikely you would ever remember what happened after you left here yesterday."

Burton picked up on the little nod from Marion which meant she had finished speaking.

He rose slowly from his chair and began, "First of all may I thank the good Lord for looking after me yesterday and also for keeping you all safe. I am sorry that I didn't explain my business in Murwillumbah but I was so upset, angry and full of guilt that I didn't want to burden anyone else. I also believed that I had a solution to my quandary and that it would be agreed to. As you all know we have been share farming with Alf Gibson at the 6 mile just over the bridge. I had invested heavily in the farm, buying extra cows and pigs as well as experimenting with the banana crop. All was looking rosy although to carry this out I had borrowed from Alf to the tune of £500. I had also used up every bit of money that I had saved over the years. If all went well we would be quite well off in two years' time."

At this point Burton stopped, took a long breath, rubbed his eyes before continuing, "Day before yesterday Alf came by. I hadn't seen him for the last 7 months. He asked how things were going and I was puffing out my chest to tell him how terrific everything was and that he would be rich in 18 months.

Alf kept avoiding my face and this was a bit annoying. He didn't sound very enthusiastic about all the things I was prattling on about. He began to walk away from me and then shocked with a loud 'I need my money back!' Well you could have knocked me over with a feather. I tried to ask him what was wrong, what I could do to clear this up, but he just kept saying over and over, 'I want my money now'. In the end he mounted his horse and as he rode away he called back 'There will be a court order at Murwillumbah for you, attend to it. Get off my land.' I was totally dumbfounded."

Burton stood still while the seconds clicked away. "I rode immediately into Murwillumbah and asked the court about an order that may have been taken by Gibson against me.

"The Clerk said Gibson had been in a week before and the order was for me to repay money owed.

"I had to give up my share of the farm as interest payable on the loan and to leave the property immediately.

"The court was in the process of issuing the order to me."

"Oh my goodness this is awful," sobbed Marion. "So what happened yesterday when you went back to Murwillumbah and why didn't you tell me what was happening?"

Burton looked at his wife and felt his heart breaking

as he plucked up the courage to tell the rest of the sordid story.

As often happens he started on the wrong foot and this didn't make him feel any more at ease. "Don't ask so many questions in one breath," he began and then immediately apologised for the sternness in his voice.

"I realised the extent of the problem after the clerk had explained that if I didn't repay the money I would be declared bankrupt."

He spat the last word out and looked upset.

"My father and grandfather all went through bankruptcy and told me it was humiliating and brought great shame on themselves and their families. I determined that I would never, ever allow that to happen to me or us."

"So what did you decide to do to solve the problem Burton?" asked Frank the youngest of the Stewarts and Marion's brother.

"Well I thought I had a clever plan but it backfired badly and left me in more trouble that I already had. On my way home from Murwillumbah I caught up with William Canter and told him of the dilemma that I was faced with. He was quick to relate a story about one of the old time farmers he knew who was faced with a similar problem. He rode like the wind back to the property rounded up all the cattle and drove them to market. The resulting money enabled him to repay his loan and all was well."

"At the time it sounded like solid advice so away I went only to find the Gibson had set up a posse to stay on the farm and make sure no one entered or touched the stock. I was done. Next I sort out William Marks the big landowner in Dunbible where my father has his farm. I asked him for a loan but when I explained the full situation he said it would be throwing good money after bad money, so he declined."

Burton stopped and took a breath before saying, "So there I was facing a court hearing in the morning and no known way to get myself out of a dastardly situation. The judge was sympathetic and even commiserated with me but in the final summing up he said that I had to repay the loan and give up my share of the property. If this could not be done then he would declare me bankrupt and send the sheriff to collect all my goods and wares. He asked me if I could pay and shamefully I replied in the negative. At that point my whole world began to swirl and I remembered calling your name Marion and begging your forgiveness. The judge said the fateful word 'Bankruptcy' and banged his gavel and I remember nothing else. We have nothing and soon the sheriff's men will arrive to collect any property we still own. I suggest we move our things to the bedroom so that Mary Jane's property is not touched."

With those instructions he slumped back in the chair and kept muttering, "I am so sorry, I am so sorry..."

The baby of the family, Keith, toddled over and

climbed up on Burton's knee and babbled, "Da, love you dada."

Mary Jane had stood stock still all the time, now she turned on her heels and with a whirl of her long white frock marched out the door.

Marion's mind was in turmoil and upon seeing her mother's demeanour she became more distressed and sobbed.

The girls, Madeline, Eva and Isobel all tiptoed out and walked solemnly towards the barn at the back of the house.

Burt, the oldest son of Burton and Marion stood his ground and tried to search in his brain for a solution.

He was not at home yesterday when all the drama was happening.

Burt had been far up the Bray's Creek cutting scrub for Uncle Hersee, who was his mother's twin brother.

His arrival home at 8.20pm was met with a barrage of stories from everyone.

Burt was tired and sore but became fully animated when he realised the seriousness of the situation.

He was devastated to hear of his father's condition.

He crept into bed determined to find a solution to whatever the problem was that confronted his father.

Marion came to her senses and became all businesslike.

She shooed Burt out the door asking him to seek out the girls and to make sure they were alright.

She picked up Keith and took him through to find his grandmother.

Mary Jane was still in a serious mood as Marion approached.

She gave the child to Mary Jane and asked if she would look after him for a while.

Mary Jane nodded and attempted to bite her tongue. She succeeded for less than the time it took for Marion to turn and reach the door.

Then Mary Jane blurted out, "I told your father he would prove to be no good!"

The he she referred to was obviously Burton.

Marion turned back to remonstrate then stopped.

It was pointless arguing with Mary Jane once she got her gander up.

Mary Jane saw the opportunity and her 5 years of pent up anger overflowed. "I said the day you brought him into the house that he would prove to be a no hoper. I've watched and started to believe that our God fearing ways would change him but no, he's always proved to be unreliable and now he's not only lost everything but he's turned to drink as well. How will God ever be able to forgive such blasphemous behaviour?"

Marion left the room.

She would have her say later when she was better composed and when they could tell her mother of their future plans.

Future plans were what she would need to seek and

her collaborator had to be her darling Burton.

She went to Burton who was still sitting on the chair where she had last seen him.

"Now my darling you need to go and rest. I'll bring you a cup of black tea and later we can talk about what we might do."

With that she helped him up and watched as he walked through to the bedroom.

The girls had reached the barn and were sitting on the milking stools talking.

Each had selected a straw from the bales of hay propped against the fence and was happily chewing the end.

Burt came whistling around the corner.

He was only ten years old but was tall and muscly.

He had been his father's little helper from a very early age and had taken on many adult responsibilities in the last year or so.

The girls all turned to him and Madeline asked the obvious question on everyone's lips, "What are we going to do now?"

Burton grabbed another stool and moved closer to the girls forming a circle.

"We pray that dad can work out something. In the meantime we need to give him and mum plenty of space. Let's get some goodies, pick up Keith and go for a picnic down at the swimming hole. This will give mum and dad a break and they will hopefully use the time fruitfully finding an answer to all our present woes."

Chapter 19

When the picnickers returned it was getting dark and the candles illuminated the rooms of the house.

They had tried to have a fun afternoon but the mood stayed sombre.

Every now and again someone would offer a solution to the family financial situation only to have the others point out the fallacies.

They trooped into the kitchen where mum and Grandma were busy making a stew. The aroma wafting through the room reminded them all that they hadn't eaten for nearly six hours.

"Off and wash up, please," commanded Grandma. "Then back here and help set the table."

They quickly carried out the instructions and after a delicious lamb stew all smothered with potatoes, onions and broad beans they retired to the lounge room.

Burt was becoming worried as he had not seen his father anywhere in the house but refrained from asking so as to not cause any angst.

Just as the work parties for cleaning away the dishes, washing up and drying were being allocated their father walked through the door.

He was full of energy and his face was far more animated than this morning.

"I think I've got it," he said as he sat down and began to take off his riding boots.

"What are you up to now Burton?" scolded Mary Jane, "Haven't you caused enough stress to last your poor family a life time?"

"Hush mum," soothed Marion, "Let's hear what Burton has got on his mind."

"I went over to Fretwell's on the other side of the Tweed and spoke to Allan Fretwell about our situation. He heard me out then said he believed he had the perfect solution. He went inside and came out with a newspaper that someone had dropped off several months ago. It was the Cairns Times and he showed me an advertisement. It was from a fellow called Lucas-Hughes who was the manager of the Australian Agricultural Group and they were seeking farmers for a new venture in a place called the Daintree. Hughes was offering a lease or share farming arrangement and in return farmers got a fully fenced 140 acres of lush dairy land, barn and a house. Everything was ready to go as there was a butter factory built and a saw mill. What an opportunity I thought. Forget all our troubles, leave them behind and start afresh. My humiliation would hopefully vanish when I tackle the new challenges. What do you say Marion?"

"Do you know where this Daintree place is and anything about it?" Marion asked.

"Fretwell said he heard a lot of talk about it. Seems it's in North Queensland and the Daintree River runs through the farming area that is in the advertisement," said Burton.

Mary Jane interrupted, "I heard about this place from one of the labourers we had a few years ago. I distinctly remember some workers and the man sitting around a campfire telling of his adventures up that way. He left me with nightmares."

"Now come on mum he probably added a bit and fabricated a lot more to embellish his stories. How else do you get people to listen? Tell them the cow was slow into the barn and no one wants to know. Tell them you had to use all six bullets in the revolver to shoot a snake when you actually, hit it over the head with a shovel and everyone is all ears," said Marion.

"That's so true." said Burton, "The men who bull-dust the best seem to get everyone's attention and they lean on it as though it was the gospel truth."

"Anyway what was he telling you and the others who were listening?" asked Marion.

Mary Jane began to relate the old man's story as best as she could recall it.

"He had been out of work for some time so he travelled north with his faithful cattle dog. He was a drover and the dog was the best in the business. He had heard of some places around Cairns where there might be work. Unfortunately he missed Cairns in his wanderings and found himself confronted by a wide impassable river. He walked along this for several miles before he came upon a humpy. He was tired and hungry so he called out and was welcomed in by a squatter. This fellow had been living in the area for a while and told him the water was the Daintree River. He said it was treacherous and contained all sorts of dangers. He named crocodiles, sharks and snakes as the worst. The drover decided the bloke was exaggerating about 20 foot crocodiles and similar sized snakes so he bid him farewell and walked on. He and the dog were over 100 yards from the river and taking in the beautiful sunset when the dog stopped and snarled. It crouched down like it was rounding up cattle or sheep. The drover threw a stick at it but the dog didn't move. Then there was a swift movement as a gigantic reptile rushed from the mangroves and rushes. It hit the dog full on and swallowed it whole. The drover ran, believing he had seen the Devil in disguise. He went south and vowed he would never go back to the Daintree ever again."

Burton sat listening to the story and now scoffed, "That's what I mean about story tellers, lots of bull-dust and very little truth. Anyway that was way before farmers moved in so I expect they have hunted out all the dangerous animals. The dairy cattle industry seems to be gathering strength in the area and I would like to give it a go. We get a 140 acre farm, a herd of cows, guarantee that our cream is bought by a Butter Factory and a house to live in. That's one offer that will set us up for the rest of our lives."

Marion's eyes lit up as Burton outlined his plans for the future but then there was a flicker of concern as she looked around at her five children.

They were so young and vulnerable, could they cope with an arduous journey and a strange new world?

She hesitated but realised Burton had already made up his mind and she had always told him how much she loved him and promised time and again to follow him to the end of the Earth.

"Yes," she simply said and the children all started cheering and hugging each other.

"We're off on a venture of a life time," shouted Madeline.

Burton's grin widened and the pressures and stress of the last few days lifted from him as he envisioned his new farm in a lush green valley flowing with cool spring water and with hundreds of cows all mooing contentedly.

The revelry was brought to a premature end when Mary Jane stepped forward and scolded, "Load of rubbish, you should know better Burton than to get your family's hopes up. You can't possibly take these little grandchildren of mine into a frightening and dangerous environment never alone expect them to trek thousands of miles to the north. You must be mad!"

With those last words she stormed out of the room and went to her bedroom.

Next morning, after the milking was done and everyone was seated around the breakfast table they heard the sound of a whip cracking and shouted commands.

Burton moved swiftly to the window and caught sight of the sheriff's dray being pulled by four horses trotting up the road.

"It's the sheriff and his sidekicks come to take our goods in default of the bankruptcy order I got. Now everyone stay calm and eat your breakfast. I'll deal with this."

The huge dray came right up to the front of the house and at the command of the tall, dark haired driver it came to a halt.

There were two out riders and one urged his horse forward and waving a sheet of paper called to Burton, "This here is a court order to repossess all of your belongings immediately."

"I know what it is and everything is in readiness for you. Take everything that is in the spare room, for that is all we own. All other articles in this house and on this land belong to Mary Jane Stewart."

"Thank you, sir for your cooperation. It is unusual for people in your predicament to be so helpful. Usually we have to argue, fight and seek out hidden items."

It took the three men very little time to collect all

the furniture and other items from the spare room and hoist them up onto the dray.

The two on horses mounted up and the dray driver took his position high up on the dray's seat and with a crack of the whip and a, "Hoy up!" they proceeded off down the road and were soon out of sight.

"Well that finishes that," said Burton as he walked back through the door into the kitchen.

Things had happened so quickly that all the children were still at breakfast.

Marion came around from where she had been sitting and put her arms around Burton's waist. "Don't worry darling we'll manage. Come, I have something important to show you."

Before either could move Mary Jane literally breezed into the room. She was all smiles and greeted all the children with a hug and a kiss on their cheeks.

Burton and Marion were startled by what was a completely different person to the one they had seen flouncing off to bed last night.

They had parted but were still standing near each other.

"And as for you two," began Mary Jane, "I wish you all the best in your new adventure. I think the change will do you all so much good."

She hardly took a breath as she raced on. "And I think I have a great idea that will help you on your way."

With those final words she sat down, winked at

Madeline and then asked of Eva, "Could you make me some breakfast this morning my lovey?"

Eva quickly set about obliging.

"What changed your mind, mother?" asked Marion, who was still in shock.

She had gone over the scenario she had expected this morning a thousand times over night.

She had hardly slept a wink as she argued back and forth from a hundred different perspectives with her mother. Now she didn't even have to think of one reason, mother had agreed to their leaving.

"I prayed to God and asked Him what He thought of my family leaving me in my old age to go off into the wilderness. He reminded me of his own son going off into the wilderness and said it had made Him into a man. I asked your father, God bless him, what he thought and he said Burton had the courage and conviction to do anything and had proven time and again he could care for his wife and children. So having heard the wise words of the two most powerful people in my life I agreed with them."

"Thanks mother," said Marion as tears welled into her beautiful aquamarine eyes.

"Come on Burton I need to show you my secret."

With that comment she put her arm around his waist and guided him from the room and into the empty spare bedroom.

The men had taken every skerrick and the room had

that hollow sound as Burton walked with his riding boots across to the window.

Marion reached her fingers to her throat and pulled on the chain of what Burton thought was a broach.

On the end, instead, was a small bag made of khaki material. The bag was pulled tight at the top and Marion wrestled with the string to get it untied.

As she did this Burton asked, "What have you here, my girl?"

"This is my little secret cache that I have been squirrelling away for a time just like we have now. Every time you have given me the house keeping I have put away a small amount. When I have done jobs like mending or washing and ironing for the workers or our neighbours I have put this away too. Now we will need every penny so that we can make the journey north to the Denmarktree."

"Daintree," corrected Burton, "You are nearly correct as a Dane does come from Denmark just like my grandfather and grandmother. So how much do we have?"

"Just over £48," said Marion proudly.

"£48," repeated Burton. "You are an absolute wonder my Marion. How did you ever think to save like that for such an emergency?"

"It was something my father would drum into us all just about every time we were given money or we earned it. 'Save a little you never know when a rainy day may come along and you will need that money'."

"Thank you, thank you," shouted Burton and he grabbed Marion around the waist with his thick muscly arms.

He lifted her off the floor and began swinging her around and around in gliding circles.

All the children rushed in to see what all the shouting was for.

Upon seeing their father and mother doing a rapid waltz they formed pairs and joined in the fun.

As they gyrated Burton called out, "Three cheers for mum she's saved the day by saving lots of money, hip pip hurray, hip pip hurray, hip pip hurray!"

Meanwhile in the kitchen Mary Jane was busy clearing away and waiting her turn to offer further good news.

As Marion and Burton came in she turned and gave them a smile. "Well I'm pleased that you took your father's advice my dear. I'm sure that money will help you a lot. However, I've been thinking what I could do to help out. Here's my part of your plan and I really hope all will go well."

She took off the apron which was a pale green with Grandma embroidered on it. It had been made by Madeline with the help of Eva especially for their grandmother. She would wear it proudly all the days of her life. It would be the one constant reminder of the darling children she would miss so much until her heart finally broke 21 years later.

"I would like to offer a number of ideas to you all so that your journey is a little easier. First Frank can take the small dray with you all on board to Murwillumbah where you can catch the ferry to Tweed heads. At Tweed Heads you board Uncle Albert's coastal ship and he will take you as far as Brisbane. From here you are going to have to work your own way to where you are going."

She couldn't bring herself to using the D word.

"Now all of this will cost money because I want you to make sure the little ones do not get exhausted with all the travelling. They should not be expected to walk at any time. They are far too young for that. So I will give you a special present which you can assume is a present for everyone's birthday and everyone's Christmas for the next ten years. I worked that out to be seven of you times two (birthday and Christmas) times £1 equals £140."

Marion gasped and her hand went first to her gaping mouth and then to stem the tears that rushed into her eyes. "That's unbelievable, mother, can you afford such generosity?"

Mary Jane was beaming with delight to see the looks of utter astonishment on the faces of the other two. "I too listened to your father's advice and agreed with his thinking. I have been saving longer than you and I've never found a rainy day to use it. Well now that day is here, take the money and my blessing and make good of yourselves."

With that she hugged both, handed Marion the purse she had been holding and went back to washing the dishes.

Chapter 20

George Whittaker was on a mission.

He had to find his way to London and then White Chapel Road where he would sign up for the adventure of a life time.

Once he signed he would be off to the wharf to board a ship to sail to Australia.

He had it all mapped out in his head. It proved to be far more difficult.

Mr Frisworth had given him instructions as to where the train station was located.

When he reached the Whyteleafe Station he was disappointed to learn from the station master that the next train to London was the morrow at 9.15 in the morning.

George resigned himself to curling up in the corner of the platform, out of the wind and weather.

He had his long coat with him but during the night even that couldn't keep out the biting cold.

He spent the rest of the five hours walking up and down the platform and hugging himself.

Eventually the train came huffing and puffing and blowing its mournful whistle.

He had a ticket so he clambered aboard and sat on the sunny side.

Whatever heat was coming through the window George desperately needed it.

London was a drab place in winter with few venturing outside unless it was essential. The smog from all the wood fires combined with the sleet that blew in every direction made it grey and dark.

George climbed from the train and went to the station ticket office to enquire as to where White Chapel Road was.

His instructions were brief and not at all easy to follow.

He tried repeating the directions hoping he would get a more detailed account but the man on the other side of the window simply dismissed him saying, "Can't you see how busy I am. Go away!"

George picked up his small brown suitcase and walked away in the direction that had been given to him.

He had to keep stopping people and asking but most were too keen to get out of the sleet and wind to be bothered giving direction to some lost boy.

Eventually luck came his way in the form of a small child. It was hard to tell the gender but George wasn't concerned all he wanted was for someone to direct him to White Chapel Road and there he would find the agent for the Australian Agriculture Group.

The small child ran up to George and tugged at his long coat. "You lost? Can I help you?"

George had been aware of pickpockets since his days in the orphanage. Many of the children incarcerated learnt to steal and the clever ones became highly efficient at picking the pockets of the supervisors and guards.

It got so bad that the manager had made it a rule that no man working in the orphanage was to carry anything of value, including food, on his person.

George stepped away from the child and pushed out his right arm. He held that position keeping the child at arm's length trying to determine how trusting he might be.

The child was unkempt, slim and wearing dirty, ripped clothing.

This brought back George's time in the orphanage when he would catch sight of the new arrivals. They would look like this urchin and would be marched off to the bath house to be scrubbed before a set of clean clothes could be found.

"Me names Bevan," said the boy holding out a grimy little hand.

"How old are you kid?"

"Six tomorra," he replied. "Don't worry, I ain't gunna rob ya. Where ya goin?"

"I need to get to White Chapel Road and you need to get out of this freezing cold. How can you bare the cold in such flimsy clothes?"

"Folla me, sir, at ya service," said the boy and he set off at a trot into the teeth of the wind.

George had little option but to run after him and hope that it wasn't a trap. He couldn't afford to lose the money he had stashed away under his clothes.

The boy pulled up ahead and pointed up to a street sign and sure enough it said White Chapel Road. "There go sir no trubl to find it."

George was so relieved and happy to be back on track.

He searched in his trouser pockets where he kept loose change and found a sixpence.

He handed it to the boy who showed genuine pleasure at such a large tip. He snatched the coin and turned to go.

A few steps later he turned back and grinned. "Ya want me to be ya guide man?"

George thought this could be an idea as the child seemed to know his way around London. "That might be a fine idea. Come on we need to find an office to the Australian Agriculture Group agent."

The search took next to no time and George was pleased to be standing in a warm, austere office facing a bespectacled man of about fifty. He was sitting behind the one piece of furniture in the room and peered at George over his thick lens glasses.

He looked at the urchin who had come in with the red headed youth and shouted, "Get out of here you."

The child turned tail and ran.

"Now young fellow, why has your father sent you on an errand to me?"

George grinned and answered, "I'm here to register to go to Australia. I have the documentation from my sponsor and I have been a farm labourer for the past 4 years."

"Name?"

"George Whittaker," he said and took out the papers he had in the pocket of his long coat.

The agent flicked through these and looked pleased. "It's a long trip son, different climate and environment to the one you're used to and it will cost you £32 to take the ship."

"Is it warm over there?" asked George knowing full well from his research what the answer would be.

"Hot as Hades so they tell me. Some days they talk about being so hot you can fry an egg on a rock."

"Then that'll do me. Anything has got to be better than being frozen for half the year," said George.

The agent accepted the fare and filled out a contract which George had to sign.

Before putting pen to the paper he read through.

The part that caught his eye and pleased him was, 'The Australian Agricultural Group guarantees a job for George Whittaker as a stockman at the Rockhampton Sales Yard'.

George happily signed.

The agent then took out a small gold card from the drawer of his desk and began to write on it. "This is your ticket so don't lose it. You give it to the captain and it tells him which cabin you are to occupy," he said.

George looked at the card as it was handed over. It had green writing for various headings and the blue ink that the agent had used to add details.

On the top was written, Australian Commonwealth Line, followed by TSS Jervis Bay; Sailing 7th January, 1926; Passenger's Name George Whittaker; Accommodation Allotted Section C Cabin 154 Berth C and at the bottom in uppercase lettering THIS CARD MUST BE SHOWN ON EMBARKATION.

George was given instructions of where to find the ship.

He thanked the agent and left.

He looked around and pulled his coat tightly around himself.

There was no sign of the young boy, Bevan.

He put his head down and trudged towards where he had seen sailing ships anchored in a river.

He reached a bridge and stood contemplating whether to cross or not.

He needed to make up his mind fast because standing still in the freezing weather was not pleasant.

George felt a light touch at the back of his coat. He flew around believing he was about to confront his first London pickpocket.

"Hi ya, what we lookin' for now?"

It was Bevan the street urchin back to be his guide.

"You're a sight for sore eyes," George said. "I need to find a ship called the Jervis Bay. She should be tied up to the wharf. All I got told by the agent was she had one funnel and it was painted orange and white."

"We finda cap'n and ask," suggested Bevan.

He set off down a flight of steps that led to the water line.

George followed and sighted ships as far as the eye could see. The boy was running towards a gang plank of an old windjammer. He was waving his arms and shouting, "Javis Bee, where's it at?"

A brawny, mountain of a man stood in the centre of the gangplank, arms folded. He looked mean and ready to toss the mite over the edge and into the muddy waters below.

The boy stopped short and repeated his question.

"Going sailing are we boy? Well you need to cross over and she's five boats downstream. She sails to Australia tomorrow on the morning tide."

"Ta much sir," said Bevan and went running back to where George was standing.

From there it was an easy walk down to the Jervis Bay.

George was amazed at how long she was and the frenetic activity on shore, on the boat and the lighters coming to and fro indicated that she was getting ready to sail.

George tossed another six pence to Bevan who

touched his forelock and said, "Thankee sir and best to ya."

Half way along the ship was a gangplank with sailors coming and going.

A tall slim man with a goatee beard was standing on the jetty side of the plank issuing orders. "Excuse me sir," called George as he approached. "I'm a paying passenger may I board?"

"Ticket, son, show me your ticket."

George readily obliged and the man looked him up and down and said, "Where are your parents?"

"I'm sailing alone, sir. I have other papers if you want to check them," offered George.

"Papers," spat the man, "That's nothing to me. Get on board and I'll have our cabin boy take you below. We sail on the tide in the morning."

A young boy of thirteen appeared at the call and said, "Follow me matey."

George struck up a conversation by asking about the ship. The young cabin boy was only too happy to give George the ship's story.

"She's a relatively new ship having been launched in 1922. She was built by the Vickers Limited shipyard at Barrow-in-Furness in England. She is 530 feet long and 68 feet at the beam. She displaces 23320 tons and has a cruising speed of 15 knots. She can carry a maximum of 723 third class passengers and 12 first class ones. She has a crew of 33."

George was impressed and then introduced himself.

The cabin boy smiled and said, "Davy at your service. Been to Australia and back three times so anything you want to know ask me or Jordy the first mate."

George found himself in a six birth cabin and chose to bunk down on a lower bed near the doorway.

He thanked Davy who said, "The mess is on the second deck forward. It has a big sign on the door. We eat breakfast at 700 hours, lunch at 1200 and dinner at 1800. Don't be late or you miss out."

George had a comfortable day exploring his new home.

He was told the journey would take about 7 weeks all going well.

That would mean arriving in Brisbane, his disembarkation port in March.

He found the galley, ate and was fast asleep by 2000 hours.

George awoke with that strange feeling he didn't know where he was. It was as if he'd been hit with a cosh rendering him unconscious and then moved to a strange location.

He opened his eyes and looked around to see he was in a ship's cabin. There was a rocking motion that was making him feel queasy.

At last he realised that he was on the Jervis Bay and that it must have been underway.

His great adventure and his future were ahead.

Chapter 21

A restless night finally dawned for the Johnson family.

They each rubbed their eyes, got up, dressed and made ready for their trip into the unknown.

They had faith in their father getting them there safely.

What they had not prepared for was the length of time and the distances they had to cover.

For their small, growing minds there was nothing more exciting than an adventure.

Of course the sadness was saying goodbye to grandma and not knowing whether they would ever see her again.

As they clambered aboard the small dray with Frank sitting high on the driver's seat they all kissed Mary Jane and said their goodbyes.

Eva, in her flippant, happy go lucky way was the one who guessed the future without realising it when she jokingly said, "See you later nan in Heaven."

They all laughed.

Everyone waved and kept waving until Mary Jane and the Bray's Creek Farmhouse disappeared from sight.

When they got to the Murwillumbah jetty they were surprised to see a crowd of people waiting. The steamer was already tethered to the wharf and the crew was busy loading crates of fowl.

As they came to a standstill and began to help everyone off the dray they heard a familiar voice shouting, "Burton, Marion over here."

There standing with about twenty other people was Grandmother Phoebe. She was Burton's mother who lived on a small dairy farm just out of Murwillumbah at a place called Dunbible.

"Ma, how did you know we were coming here or was it just a coincidence?" called Burton.

The portly, grey haired woman tapped her finger to her nose to indicate a secret.

Her wrinkled face broke into a wide grin as she was mobbed by five exuberant children.

"Nana, nana," they chorused in unison.

She reached into her pocket and pulled out five boiled lollies. The green one went to Madeline, a red one to Isobel, yellow to Burton, an orange one for little Keith and for her favourite it was black to Eva. They began sucking on the sweet knowing that it would last for nearly an hour as long as they didn't chew it or it had those dreaded air pockets inside.

"I came to say goodbye. I couldn't let you sneak off like a thief in the night now could I?"

The hidden meaning was not lost on Burton and he began to stammer an excuse and changed his thoughts to a different one and eventually got tongue tied.

"No matter Burton I have always trusted your judgements so I can only wish you the best and hope you stay healthy and safe. Look after these beautiful grandkids of mine."

The boat siren gave out its mournful call and Marion began to usher the children towards the gangplank.

The goodbyes and tears flowed as free as the water in the Tweed River.

They finally clambered aboard and the crew cast off the mooring ropes.

They were on their way.

They waved and called out and the people on shore got tinier and tinier and then disappeared as the boat rounded a curve.

Chapter 22

The Jervis Bay had been built for the long haul trips between England and Australia.

Assisted passengers were paid their fare to migrate to Australia to boost the labour force especially in the pastoral industries.

England had a glut of workers and was only too keen to encourage people to migrate to one of their dominions.

The swell across the Bay of Biscay was enormous and George soon discovered that he didn't have his sea legs as yet.

Many of the other passengers were also feeling unwell and the noise of vomiting could be heard throughout the vessel day and night.

The sea calmed considerably as the Jervis Bay turned to port and sailed through the Strait of Gibraltar and out into the Mediterranean Sea.

For the first time in three days George was able to leave his bed and go on deck.

There was a slight breeze blowing from the north and the sea was emerald green.

All about were sailing craft and he could see land to the north and south.

"That's the Rock of Gibraltar over there," said a familiar voice.

George turned from the railing and faced Davy. "And on the other side is North Africa or more to the point Morocco."

George was fascinated by all these strange names. "How do you remember all the places and their names?"

"When you see them as often as I have and you are asked by everyone on the ship it's not easy to forget," said Davy.

The land receded and George marvelled at the expanse of the Mediterranean Sea. He recalled seeing a World globe at the orphanage that one of the supervisors had brought in. One of the places he had pointed out was this vast sea. Now George was sailing across it.

After two days land was seen dead ahead or east as Davy pointed out.

He said the ship was approaching the Suez Canal. This was a short cut to the Indian Ocean.

"The first man to find a way by to the Spice Islands, or the East Indies was a bloke called Vasco Da Gama. He set sail from Portugal and went south along the African coast. When he got to the Cape of Good Hope he turned north and hugged the coast until he reached Columbo in Ceylon. From there it was easy sailing to Djakarta.

"Now we can do the trip in an eighth of the time by going through the Suez Canal."

"The Sue's what?" asked George.

"The Suez with a z as in buzz was dug through the Isthmus of Suez so that ships could get to the Indian Ocean quickly. They started digging it by hand in 1859. Now it is a waterway from the Mediterranean Sea to the Indian Ocean."

George was standing with Davy leaning on the railing watching other ships slip slowly passed.

Behind them he could see another sailing vessel. "Seems pretty busy," he said.

"All the shipping from Europe to Asia, Australia and New Zealand come this way," said Davy.

It took most of the day to navigate through the canal and by evening they were facing the huge expanse of water called the Indian Ocean.

The First Mate began to collect groups of people together and offer them information about the places they were going to in Australia.

His first group was formed of those who were disembarking in Perth.

Davy explained to George that because he was headed to Brisbane his talks would take place after they visited Sydney and that was a long way off yet.

The weather was hot and still and the British passengers found the change too sudden. They would sprawl around the deck trying to lay in the shade and catch a breath of air.

Many of the ladies resorted to rolling their dresses up to their knees and draping their feet out through the railing. This was most unladylike but the captain and crew turned a blind eye as they had seen this happen many times.

On the third week after leaving the Suez Canal there was a lot of chatter and pointing among the crew.

George sought out Davy to find out what the concern was. "Storm clouds on the north-eastern horizon could spell trouble," said Davy.

"We are at that time of the year when the monsoons hit this area. These are very strong winds and torrential rain.

"We hit one last year about March and it belted us for five days and nights. The scariest I have ever seen. Hopefully we can out run this one by heading due south."

A few days later and the boatswain was running around the ship holding a hand written sign. On it were the words 'Crossing the Equator'.

This was greeted with people calling out and giving each other hugs.

George had not had any time to think about girls up to this time in his life. Their lack in his first 15 years of life meant he had not developed any passion or interest in the opposite sex. So when one forward young blond gave him a hug and a wet peck on the cheek he merely said, "Thanks miss."

The storm did not eventuate to everyone's relief.

However there was a weird incident that kept the passengers guessing and gossiping.

It started one morning around 1100 hours when all passengers were called by the crew to assemble on deck.

The urgency in the calling out by the crew members had some believing the ship was to be abandoned.

There was some panic and one elderly lady collapsed and had to be attended to by the ship's doctor.

The captain had split the crew into working groups of four to cover all the 700 plus passengers.

George was lucky in that he was with Davy and three others so he was getting his information first hand.

The captain was of the belief that there was a stow-away on board and it was essential he be caught and returned to his port of embarkation.

All the passengers were to be sent to their cabins and were to remain there.

A blast on the ship's horn would start the search and another would end it.

A loud mournful honk sent the passengers to their quarters.

For the next three hours everyone waited for the ship to be searched.

Finally the blast everyone was waiting for and

passengers scurried onto the deck gasping for fresh cool air.

Davy found George lying on the deck looking up at the moon which had made an early appearance.

"We found the blighter, he was hiding in the life-boat aft," said Davy pointing to the back of the ship.

"The captain got onto him because the cook kept missing things from the galley. The Boatswain found a piece of bread and half a sausage on the deck below one of the other lifeboats so they determined we had to have an extra passenger.

"To find him was difficult but by locking everyone in we could make an easy clean sweep of the entire ship.

"Poor bloke will be put off at Fremantle next week and then another ship will take him back to London.

"His name's Jack Bryatt and he's been hiding since we left England. Must have wanted to run away real bad."

Fremantle came into sight with several islands off the starboard side before the ship entered the port itself.

There were hundreds of people lining the wharf and calling to those on board who were preparing to leave.

Two policemen dressed in dark blue and with caps on their heads climbed on board and poor Jack Bryatt the stowaway was put in handcuffs and man-handled from the ship. It was a sad sight for all who knew his story.

The turnaround was less than four hours and George and the remaining passengers were sailing out of Fremantle heading for the rough seas of the Great Australian Bight.

For four days the ship fought against howling winds and monstrous seas.

A freezing southerly added to the discomfort although many of the ex-British passengers thought they were back in England.

On the fifth day the Jervis Bay sailed into Port Phillip Bay and there dead ahead of the ship they were able to see the city of Melbourne.

Again those disembarking were sent off down the gangplank and the ship sailed out headed for Sydney.

George was in awe of the Sydney Heads when the ship reached them. They towered way over the ship and the gap seemed tiny compared with the expanse of water they saw in Sydney Harbour itself.

The ship made all haste for a wharf which Davy had great delight in spelling and then asking George to say the word. George tried and this started Davy giggly to the point that he couldn't stop.

"Come on George it's not that hard to say Woolloomooloo!"

The passengers disembarking were soon walking down the gangplank.

Some were met by relatives and friends, others just stood looking bewildered by their strange new land.

The Jervis Bay sailed on the tide next day with the next stop to be Brisbane.

George was becoming excited and apprehensive as he tried to image what lay ahead.

The First Mate had called the remaining passengers together and spoke to them about what to expect in Brisbane and Queensland.

He spent some time on dangerous creatures and what to do if you were bitten by the deadly taipan, death adder, king brown and the like or the red back or funnel web spider.

He also told them about crocodiles that inhabited some or the rivers and estuaries in north Queensland.

His talks were informative and well received.

The most important point he made was, "Most of the people you will meet and do business with are the same as you. They have taken a boat voyage from their birth land to Australia to start a new life. So they will be as eager to help you as you will be to meet them."

Brisbane proved to be a river port which surprised George as all the other ports they had visited were all on the coast.

The Brisbane River was tiny like the Thames and the trip from the sea took nearly three hours due to the crowded water way and the need for careful navigation.

The wharf was busy and it took a lot of manoeuvring to finally anchor the ship.

George said his teary goodbye to Davy and wished him well. "No doubt you'll be a ship's captain the next time we meet," he said.

"And you a big time, rich landowner," said Davy.

George clambered down the gangplank, turned and waved and set off to his next adventure.

He had to find a way to a place called Rockhampton because that is where he would find his new job.

It had become evident that all coastal movement was by boat.

He began asking those he met if they knew of any ship sailing north to Rockhampton.

It didn't take long before someone pointed him in the direction of a small fishing boat. "That's the one mate she's on her way back north. It will land you there tomorrow morning."

Chapter 23

The trip from the Pacific Ocean up the Fitzroy River for the Johnson family was a Godsend after nearly six days of topsy turvy swell and lots of sea sick passengers.

They had made it to the Tweed Heads and from there it was rough weather to Brisbane and rougher still to Rockhampton.

Each of the children had a bout of sea sickness lasting from a few hours to a day or two.

Burton found his sea legs quickly but Marion was stricken for the entire journey.

To Madeline it was quite odd because she was in charge of nursing her mother while Eva took care of little Keith. Madeline was mystified by the fact that mum was more unwell in the mornings than any other time. She found herself emptying the sick bucket two or three times first thing in the mornings but only once across the day and night.

Now they all stood at the front of the ship as she chugged her way up the flat Fitzroy River. On each side the banks were entangled with mangroves and thick scrub grew beyond.

The town of Rockhampton was over 15 miles from the ocean. It was a trading centre for the sheep and cattle stations of the inland of Queensland. This information had come via a passenger, Mr Longines who was a buyer and seller of animals for the meat industry.

He had also been full of information for Burton in regards to the Daintree River and the area being opened up for dairy farmers.

Mr Longines had said he knew Lucas-Hughes, the man managing the project and often ran into him at a Hotel in Rockhampton. This gave great heart to Burton as it would make it easy for him to strike a deal.

The Rockhampton Wharf was a busy place and the captain of their vessel had to use all his skill to berth.

Once the space was found and the ship settled against the timber dock the crew secured the lines forward and aft.

A gangplank was placed in position and the captain made a loud announcement. "All women and children alight then gentlemen you can pick up your luggage and leave the ship."

Madeline put her arm around her mother's waist and they shuffled across the gangplank and onto solid earth.

For Marion the rocking continued and it would be several days before the oozy feeling would finally cease.

All the others were shepherded by Burt.

They waited patiently for Burton to join them.

They walked along the side of the river following the other passengers who had disembarked. Burton said that someone would know how to get into town so follow the leader and sure enough they soon found themselves turning into a street full of shops and hotels.

One hotel stood out from the rest. It had a large sign above the second floor announcing Leichardt Hotel.

Burton pointed out the entrance and said, "Right this looks good we'll stay here until I find Mr Hughes."

He made his way to the front counter behind which stood a lad dressed in red and black uniform with a bellboy hat on.

"Excuse me?" said Burton, "Can I get some rooms for a day or two?"

The boy looked up and nodded before turning towards an open door at the back of the office and called, "Customers mum, a whole big damn heap of 'em."

A short, stout lady with greying hair appeared at the doorway. She moved remarkably fast considering her stature and was all business. "Names Mary Jones, now how many we got here sir?"

"Just the Mrs and myself and five children madam," replied Burton.

"We'll make that two rooms, a double for you, the little lady and baby. As long as you keep the rest under control they can bunk in another room. Any nonsense or loud noise, arguing, swearing, drunkenness then you're all out. That will be £2 for the two days. You want an extension it will be a £1 for each day extra. Take it or leave it I'm a busy woman."

"We'll take it and I can assure you everyone will be nice and sensible and quiet," replied Burton.

"Yeah they all say that but then I have to stick my bib in and they don't like that so I then have to turf them out. Rooms 13 and 14, up the stairs turn right and should be fourth door on the left. Jack here will help show you the way. Keys are for you sir look after them and leave them at the front desk if you're going out."

All the time she had been talking she also wrote the details in a book. As the family started to move upstairs she thumped her head with a chubby hand and exclaimed, "What name am I dealing with here and I need the £2 up front."

"Johnson," replied Burton, and then began to slowly spell it for her, "J-O-H-N-S-O-N."

It didn't take long for everyone to choose a bed and pile their meagre belongings at the end.

They all eagerly ran into their parents' room and began to beg for a tour of the town.

"Please dad can you show us around and maybe we can get something to eat. I'm starving now that the rocking has stopped," said Eva.

Everyone agreed with her thinking except Marion. She struggled to stand up and kept sitting on the bed.

Eventually she lay down and said to Burton, "Take the children on a tour of Rockhampton my dear and I'll stay and look after Keith."

Madeline was quick to offer to stay with her just in

case she needed something or Keith became upset.

"I'll be alright. I have been looking after all of you when I have been a lot worse than I am now."

So it was decided and the happy party set off downstairs and out into the busy street.

They walked along window shopping and were amazed at what was on offer in a town that seemed to be so far from any other place on earth.

The wide dusty streets seemed to go on forever no matter which one you walked along.

There was one steel bridge that went across the Fitzroy River. They had passed under this in the morning as they came up the river.

As they walked the sun began to appear as it had been quite overcast on their trip up the river.

From a distance they could hear the lowing of cattle.

As they moved in the direction of the sounds the noise got louder. They found themselves standing outside the biggest saleyards in Australia. Yards stretched in every direction for miles. So this was where Mr Longines would be doing his business.

Burton wondered if he would find Lucas-Hughes here as well.

A cheery English voice called out to them, "Hello folks I'm George can I be of assistance you look a little lost?"

They looked up and there on the top of the wooden fence, perfectly balanced was a boy of fifteen or sixteen.

He was so skinny that mum would have sat him down and fed him two helpings of her special stew. He was dressed in work overalls with straps tied at the shoulder.

What caught all their attention and would become etched in their minds forever was the bright ginger mop of hair on his head. It was the brightest ginger any of them had ever seen.

Chapter 24

Burton was the first to speak, "We're visitors from the south and we were following this road and found the sales yard. I'm Burton Johnson and these are my children. What might I ask are you doing perched up there?"

"Introduce me to you kids and I'll take you on a quick tour if you would like that."

Apart from the word kid he had a cultured voice that gave the impression of one well educated. They would find out later that that was not entirely the case.

George jumped down from the fence and landed cat like beside them. "Follow me," he said and swept his arm in a round motion and pointed ahead.

Everyone fell in behind him and he was like a Pied Piper dragging the mesmerised children into his trap.

George was so knowledgeable and entertaining.

He pointed out things and threw statistics at the group all the while laughing at his own jokes.

After nearly an hour they were all thoroughly versed in the way the sales yard worked and what each and every man's job entailed.

It was now late in the afternoon so Burton called a halt to the sightseeing and thanked George for his time.

He turned to the children and had them chorus a thank you as well.

As they all departed Burton asked George, "Where do you stay son?"

George, eager as ever, explained that he was staying with a widow out along the main road. The house was on a couple of acres and was all that was left of the woman's husband's farm. It still had the barn out the back but it was no longer in use.

At the front was a huge almond tree that was presently full of white blossom. She had been grateful to have George billeted as he was company for her and did lots of odd jobs. The money he paid in board came in handy to her.

They all reached the hotel, tired, hungry and thirsty.

Marion was up and about and in her wisdom had already organised for them all to have dinner in the hotel lounge.

She had them wash their hands and faces and then troop downstairs.

As Isobel said as she swallowed her last mouthful of ice-cream, "That was the best meal I've ever had."

Burton saw them all off to their rooms and kissed Marion goodnight before explaining that he was going to make enquiries about Lucas-Hughes. He was sure someone would know him and know his whereabouts.

Unaccustomed to bars as he was it took quite an effort for Burton to enter the saloon.

The stale smell of beer and the billowing of cigarette smoke did not help.

He braced himself and sort out men who looked like cattleman. Rough and loud and clothed with riding gear were the indicators he used.

His enquiry of Lucas-Hughes met with a lot of head shaking and it didn't take long before he had covered the entire population of the bar including the barman.

Disappointed and becoming tired after his long voyage and full day he retired to bed.

Marion was already asleep.

He was pleased to note that her sick bowl was empty for the first time in over a week.

He should have known better, after all he was the father of five children. It just didn't seem to click even when all the signs were staring him in the face.

He awoke with a jolt, it was pitch dark and he seemed lost in a strange room. He reached for the switch above his bed but banged something else which hurt his hand.

He caught the sound of someone vomiting near him then realised it was Marion.

"I thought she was over this?" he said to himself.

She heaved again and began to dry wrench.

"You alright dear,?" he asked soothingly.

"Oh Lord help me," begged Marion and she heaved again.

The light flickered on and Madeline ran to her mother's side.

"There, there mum take it easy, have a sip of water and rinse your mouth. That's the way."

She spoke reassuringly and soon Marion settled back on the pillow and said, "Thanks sweetie you are so kind to me."

"I thought we had gotten over this now we're off the ship," said Burton.

Madeline raised her dark eyebrow above her right eye and began to giggle. "You want me to tell him mum or are you going to do it?"

Marion put a hand over her mouth and gestured with the other for Madeline to go ahead.

"Haven't you worked it out dad? Mum is very sick in the mornings and continues to be so even though we aren't on the rocky ship anymore. Morning Sickness means..?" She left the sentence unfinished.

The new baby was some months away from being born but had caused a huge change of plans.

Marion was in no fit state to continue the journey, they needed a cheaper place to stay, Burton needed a job as the money was slowly being spent, Lucas-Hughes was nowhere to be found.

Burton began to frequent places he believed he would run into local farmers looking for a farm labourer.

He went into the many hotels in Rockhampton and always approached the barman first.

He was the ears of the establishment and the one who would likely know most of the men who drank at his bar.

After making his enquiry and getting a negative reply he would ask the barman to keep an ear out for a possible labouring job. He explained he was staying at the Leichardt and gave them his room number.

He went off to the sales yards and asked around, following the crowd who followed the auctioneer.

Between breaks when the men were moving between pens he would casually introduce himself and ask for work.

Each in turn would listen politely but shake their heads, promising to keep an ear to the ground.

At the end of the day, tired and disappointed Burton would make his way back to the quiet and comfort of his hotel room. Here, Marion would be waiting with a hot cup of black tea at the ready and a kiss to soothe his disappointments.

On the fourth day that the family had been in Rockhampton Marion was surprised to hear a loud knock on the door of their room.

Burton had already been gone for several hours and the children had gone off to walk along the riverfront. Burt and Madeline had suggested this idea so as to give their mother some welcome quiet time.

Marion eased herself into a sitting position, swung

her feet off the mattress and stood up.

She called as she walked, "Hold on please I'm coming."

She opened the door and there stood a boy of about seven.

"Sorry to bother you miss, message for Mr Johnson."

He opened his sweating fingers of his right hand and held in his dusty palm a crumpled piece of paper."

Marion took the scrap and unfolded it.

She was so excited that she moved forward to give the boy a hug, thought better of it, fumbled in her dress pocket and found a sixpence which she handed to him. "Thanks ever so much," she said.

"Much obliged," replied the boy before he scampered away.

Marion waited throughout the rest of the day hardly able to contain herself.

When the children returned she didn't tell them about the note but she did feel like rushing out to find Burton to tell him the news.

She knew this would be a fruitless search as she had no idea where he was.

At precisely six o'clock he came through the door, removed his hat from his rudy forehead and spun it towards the hat stand. As always, it missed and landed at Marion's feet. She bent automatically, picked it up and put it on the protruding metal hook.

"Have I got some pleasant news for you," she said as she moved towards him and kissed his cheek, feeling the salty perspiration on her lips.

She handed him the note and waited in anticipation of another waltz.

As predictable as ever, Burton let out a whoop, grabbed her around the waist, lifted her off her feet and began to spin her around.

The children filed into the room, having heard their father's cry of delight.

They were eager to hear his good news, for he only ever whooped like that when something really fantastic had happened.

"I've got me a job," he called, "Not just any job, this one is a job a man waits all his life for."

He put Marion down near the bed and assisted her to sit down.

He gestured to the children to sit and they all obeyed.

Burton then held up the piece of paper and read, "Mr Johnson, need share farmer, Geo Sirrat pen 27 tom 6. For your information that means that Mr George Sirrat, one of the most innovative farmers in the Rockhampton district wants to offer me a partnership in his farm. He wants me to meet him tomorrow morning at 6 am at the sale yards pen 27."

Everyone was so pleased they began to cheer and slap each other on the back.

Silence was swift and the crowd brought under control when a loud voice called from the door, "Stop this racket before I toss you all out in the street."

It was Mrs Jones the proprietor.

Next morning Burton was up early having spent a restless night. He kept going over in his head what Mr Sirrat would be like, what the farm would be like, what clever ideas he could put in place, how much… the list was not only endless but he went over each item time and again.

Thank goodness the sun had finally risen and the clock hands had ticked to the ten and five position.

He dressed quickly and had seven minutes to make the rendezvous.

He hurried out the door and down the stairs.

The crisp morning air was a welcome relief after the stuffiness of the hotel room. He would be glad to get out onto the land again and do what he was best at.

As he approached pen 27 he could hear the auctioneer calling his prices. He was rapid fire as the farmers bid at single prices for the animals that were in the pen. It didn't matter how many animals made up the lot you bid for one but then multiplied that by the total animals yarded to get the full price you had to pay.

Young George, the lad with the bright ginger hair, had carefully explained that the other day when he had given them their own special tour of the sale yards.

A stout man about five feet nine stood near pen 27 as Burton approached.

He took a watch from his fob pocket, expertly spinning it on a gold chain before catching it and glancing at the face.

Burton called out, "Burton Johnson, sir are you waiting for me?" He used this approach so as to not cause any embarrassment if the stranger was not who he thought he was.

Chapter 25

The stout gentleman in the grey attire turned and grinned. "Very punctual, Mr Johnson, I like a man who is always on time and ready to get down to business. Most impressive I must say."

With that start Burton was beaming.

"Name's George Sirrat and I own several farms out west of here. I have small acreage out at Mt Larcom some fifteen miles away and am determined to turn it into a model dairy farm. I've only just purchased the land but it has all the attributes I believe it needs to be a classic dairy property. With prices for milk edging towards a shilling I believe we could make a killing."

Burton had not interrupted at any point while George Sirrat was explaining his ambitions. He was pleasantly pleased to hear his inclusion towards the end of the information sharing.

"Well son what do you think? You haven't said a word are you as good at this dairying as you've been sprouting all round town or is it all hot air like most of the others I've had the misfortune to run into?"

"Oh no, sir you are looking at one of the best and innovated dairy farmers from the south. I've spent the past 20 years perfecting my trade.

"I like to believe that I'm a dairy and mixed farmer as I see so much in dairying that you can use in raising other animals and crops rather than wasting produce or having to buy in feed."

George Sirrat's face lit with a wry smile.

He was clearly pleased to not only hear what was just said but he was pleased with the physical stature of the man standing in front of him.

Clearly this tall, red-haired man had toiled long and hard in the hot boiling Australian sun. His muscles bulged from under his white, long sleeved shirt and he held himself upright. The confidence in his voice and his words were enough to seal the deal.

"I'll send a wagon around to the Leichardt at ten and the driver will convey you to 'Cassowary' where you will find a comfortable homestead and my overseer waiting to help you get settled in. Tomorrow at six in the morning I will visit and we'll discuss how we are going to operate and also discuss the financial side of the business. Thank you for your time Mr Johnson, until tomorrow, farewell."

True to his word the buckboard and driver pulled up at the entrance to the Leichardt Hotel at 10 sharp.

The Johnson family were there earlier all anticipating the next adventure in their young lives.

This had not been on their itinerary but when Burton had explained everything last night they knew it was necessary and hopefully short term in the overall plan.

The buckboard was pulled by two fine, bay horses, well groomed and with a flash of white down the forehead to the nostrils.

Eva had been the one to notice the striking resemblance and suggested they were twins.

The driver, a seemingly bright young man all decked out in his town attire was taken by the comment but corrected it to, "No miss not twins but close. They have the same mum and dad but are a year apart."

The horses set off at a trot urged on by the driver and they were soon out in the countryside.

Burton, sitting up on the seat beside the driver, was especially pleased. He beamed from one side of his face to the other as he breathed in the clean air and pointed out land marks to the children in the back.

After nearly half an hour the driver turned the buckboard off the main track and made his way towards a large stone building. It had a tall windmill out to one side and four chimneys protruding from the red tiled roof.

"Here you are sir," said the driver, "This is Cassowary Station. Well part of it. Mr Sirrat bought only the house paddock section from old man Thompson a few months ago. He's talking about turning it into a dairy farm so I suppose that's where you folk come in."

After unloading the family settled into what proved to be a rambling house with five bedrooms. It also had all the modern conveniences of that time.

Burton called them all to a meeting on the verandah.

The view was quite spectacular. Looking across lush, green pastures one could make out a creek flowing gently passed and then further off were remnants of the forest that once covered the entire area. Further away still were the mountains rising spectacularly from the plain. This panorama was repeated as they walked around the verandah that swept all the way around the house.

It was Madeline who voiced what everyone was thinking, "It looks almost like home back in Bray's Creek."

The house itself was built on the English style, made of stones laid by a skilled craftsman. The verandah was an Australian idea to allow more shade on the main house and give relief from the searing heat of summers. It also increased the roof area so that more rain could be run off into the large corrugated iron tanks that seemed to lurk in each corner.

Unlike the new Queenslander houses, that were springing up everywhere in this part of the country, it did not have the high stumps that allowed breezes to flow through underneath. The other difference is it was not made of timber.

"Well this is home for the foreseeable future so make yourselves comfortable. Tomorrow we shall see what Mr Sirrat has in store for us. We'd better be very careful as I don't want a repeat of what happened in my last share farming venture," said Burton.

Precision was a trait of Mr Sirrat that they would have to get used to. Horse and rider pulled up at the hitching rail at exactly 6 the next morning.

Marion had seen him riding in along the track to the homestead and had called out to Burton and the children.

Everyone was spruced up, dressed in their best clothes and ready to meet the new 'boss'.

Mr Sirrat was warm in his greeting to them all and asked after their well-being.

He was happy to be introduced to each of the family and to enjoy a cup of tea.

Once the preliminaries were over, however, he became all businesslike.

He took Burton aside and as they strolled around the barn and across the paddocks he explained what his vision for his dairy farm entailed. Burton was enthralled by the clearness with which Mr Sirrat outlined his ideas.

Once they were back at the homestead and eaten a lovely morning tea of scones and jam the two men retired to the study to thrash out the financial arrangements.

The basic arrangement was for Burton to farm the land as a dairy and to sell the produce. He was to make all the necessary changes and build whatever he believed he needed to make the farm flourish over the next few months.

Mr Sirrat would fund all the things that were bought or built as long as Burton explained the necessity of such expenditure.

Burton and the family would be required to work the farm with 33% of the profit being theirs to keep.

Burton was pleased with these arrangements but insisted on a rider at the bottom of the contract that Mr Sirrat had written. This added note indicated that at no stage during the four month period could Mr Sirrat remove the family from the property unless they committed heinous crimes.

Mr Sirrat heard Burton's story and shaking his head said, "I have heard of this happening all too often. You have my word Burton that you will be well thought of here and I know I will end up with the best modern dairy in Rockhampton."

After signatures were scrawled at the bottom of the contract page the two men shook hands.

They both laughed and slapped each other on the back.

Now it was up to Burton to show what he was capable of.

Within a week the farm had 40 head of cows and a well organised milking shed.

The children were all put to work milking morning and evening, something they were used to.

George Whittaker or Ginger as he had now been nicknamed was hired to cart the milk into Rockhampton each morning. Pick up time was five thirty and the ten cans were made up of evening milking and the morning milking.

Burton then set about building a piggery and bought six sows and Mr Sirrat bought a prize boar from a neighbour. This rather huge black pig had won first prize at the Malinda Show recently so was well bred.

Another of Mr Sirrat's traits was that he only bought the best breeding stock.

It would take a few weeks before two beautifully bred bulls turned up. These were originally from California. Mr Sirrat had bought them three years ago when the first embryo of his dairy farm was formed. They were showing their ability to breed cows with twice the milk output of the usual ones everyone had.

Mr Sirrat had bred these with a variety of his cows and was pleased with the results. He now told Burton to use these as his breeders for the cows on the farm.

The two huge bulls were accompanied by six heifers that were their offspring.

Mr Sirrat wanted to keep them all together as he intended to enter them in a district show in a few months' time.

He asked Burton to take them in hand and bring

them up to show standard.

Burton was by now working a full sixteen hours a day and enjoying it immensely.

He could not believe that he was getting so much information about dairy farming, breeding and learning new skills every day.

Once he got to the Daintree and took over his own farm he could put all this learning into his own enterprise.

Unfortunately he had not learnt the hard lessons of yesteryear especially the one that warned, 'Beware of those things coming out of left field – things you never ever would expect under normal circumstances.'

Burton continued to toil day and night, seven days a week. He had added a fowl run to the farm for eggs and had ploughed an area for vegetables to be grown. He left Marion to ensure the plants were watered daily and she was in charge of picking anything needed for meals.

He rotated the cows into different paddocks and when he found there were not enough fields he built new fences limiting each to 40 acres.

The bulls were kept separate from the cows until they were required to be mated with the selected cows. Only five cows every four months so that milking would be maintained at a maximum.

Burton also ploughed one of the paddocks using a horse and double farrowed plough.

As with everything on a farm it was exhausting work.

He sowed this with oats so that once the crop was harvested it would provide hay and oats as feed to the animals on the farm.

He was developing his mixed farm where each part integrated and complemented each other part.

Mr Sirrat was overjoyed that he had found a hard-working and progressive farmer.

He had sidled up to Burton one day and handed him a plain envelope saying, "This is a little bonus Burton to show how pleased I am. Our next contract will be for five years if that's what you want."

He had then climbed onto his horse and rode away.

As Burton watched the figure slowly disappear he opened the envelope and there he counted £120 all in crisp £20 notes.

When he looked up again the rider was gone and this was an ominous warning that failed to take root in Burton's mind as he was so happy.

Chapter 26

The family had been on the farm for three months and 22 days at the time Mr Sirrat had paid them a visit and left the bonus. A new contract would soon be needed.

Marion was showing and according to her dates she was well into the eighth month and excitedly awaiting the birth of her sixth child.

She never had had any problems with the birth of her children and didn't expect any this time.

The distance to Rockhampton was the main concern so she had decided to pack a bag or two in readiness.

She even considered going in and staying with Miss Becky who was the lovely spinster who billeted Ginger.

She owned a couple of acres and a small cottage two miles out of Rockhampton and less than a mile from the hospital.

Miss Becky had a spare room as Ginger bunked down on the enclosed verandah at the back. He found this more comfortable as he could open all the louvres and get a nice breeze through keeping even the hottest nights cooler.

It was the next day when young 11 year old Burt noticed a group of rider and a gig coming along the main road.

He was out checking on a fence that seemed to have been broken because the cows had been found in the wrong field this morning.

Milking was in no way delayed as the two boys, Ginger and Burt, were quick to locate them and drive them to the barn. After discussing the problem with his father, Burt had saddled the farm horse, Horatio and ridden off to locate the break.

As he took his concentration back to the broken fence he noticed a tree had fallen over ahead. Sure enough the tree had squashed the wires and snapped the top two. This had created a low point for the cattle wandering passed and looking for some way to get into the paddock next to the one they were grazing in.

"The grass is always greener on the other side of the fence," mused Burt as he dismounted. He took to the tree trunk with an axe he carried in the saddle, heaved each part away from the fence.

Using some spare wire and a pair of pliers he soon had the break mended.

Satisfied he headed back to the homestead to make his report.

His approach to the house was from the back so nothing seemed to be out of the ordinary.

As he came nearer he could hear raised voices, one of which oddly was his father's.

He dug his boots into Horatio's ribs and the horse

responded into a canter.

As he rounded the side of the house he could see two horseman seated on their mounts in front of Burton.

Another man was standing chest to chest with his father and they were shouting into each other's face.

A small, petite woman was seated in the gig holding the reins in her right hand. She had a parasol in her left to shade her from the heat of the noon day sun.

"...twenty four hours and that's it!" were the last words Burt heard as he reined in his horse next to his father.

He had intended to ride between the two arguing men which was a game thing to do by an eleven year old.

He was shocked to believe anyone would have to argue with his father or to make threats and he certainly didn't want anyone getting physical towards him.

The angry man climbed into the gig, snatched the reins from the young lady, flicked them across the back of the horse and galloped away. The two mounted men made to follow when one turned back and added loudly, "When we come back you'd be well off or we won't be so pleasant."

They galloped off and soon disappeared into the dust stirred up by the racing gig.

"What was that all about?" asked Burt as he dismounted from Horatio.

"Mr Sirrat is dead," said Burton painfully and

seemed to miss his son's question. "I don't believe it. He apparently was riding home and nearly there when his manager saw him stop and fall from his horse. By the time they got to him he had suffered a heart attack and passed away. Oh the poor fellow he was so genuine not like that rabble that just rode out."

"Oh dad I'm so sorry to hear about Mr Sirrat. What will we do now?" asked Burt. Then as an afterthought he again asked, "Who was that you were arguing with?"

"That was Robert Sirrat in the gig and his other two brothers Will and Colin. They are the rest of Mr Sirrat's family. I have never met them until today but I was warned that they were bad news. Mr Sirrat had shielded us from them but now he is gone."

At this point he stopped and took his handkerchief from his pocket and wiped away tears welling into both eyes.

He cleared his throat and continued, "Come on son we'd better sit everyone down and tell them what has happened."

Marion and the other children were soon in the lounge room waiting expectantly to hear what all the yelling had been about and why four strange people had visited the farm.

Near the front door Ginger waited ready to be told to leave.

Surprisingly Burton addressed him first when he came into the room. "I'm glad you're still here son because I have an important job for you."

He turned to the family and looking from one to the other began to explain what had recently taken place out the front of the homestead.

"The visitors we just had were the other Sirrat family members. They are Mr Sirrat's brothers and the woman was a wife of one of them. The very bad news is that Mr Sirrat has passed away. It seems he was riding home last evening when he took ill and fell from his horse. When others found him he had died of a heart attack. This leaves us in a very bad situation because his brothers are demanding that we leave immediately and that they will no longer accept the contract we have. If we do this we will leave with very little and all the hard work we have put into the extras on the farm will be forfeited to the money hungry Sirrats."

At this point Burton took a breath and sat down on the spacious lounge next to Marion.

She instinctly reached across and gave him a cuddle, "We'll be alright my darling you wait and see."

"Now we haven't any time to grieve for Mr Sirrat. We need to get everything packed and be out of here by nightfall. I know I'm asking a lot but you can do this. Ginger, I want you and Burt to join me, immediately we finish here, in the barn. We have some urgent business with the Thompsons over the other side of the valley. Marion I'm going to leave you in charge of the packing and moving. Madeline can organise the working parties and she can drive the buckboard into town. When you get there go to the Leichardt and book a room for the night. Tomorrow morning I will be there before 5 o'clock so I want everyone dressed and ready to move. No questions asked, please. Now let's act."

With those final words he bounded out of the chair and strode across the room for the front door.

Ginger swung the door open and followed Burton out across the verandah.

Burt ran to catch up and the last Marion saw of them was Burton with his arms around each of the boys' shoulders disappearing into the barn.

Marion struggled to place herself into a position where she was sitting on the edge of the lounge. She heaved herself up and stood holding her back. Her distended tummy showed she was well advanced with the pregnancy.

She was hoping for a boy to even the genders up but one had to wait for what God had designed. No point in wishing or hoping when things had already been put in place.

It was just after 12 noon when the frenetic activity started. It was surprising how well organised the packing went.

By four thirty the family was assembled on the verandah.

In front of them was the buckboard and the two bay horses ready to take them into Rockhampton.

Once there they would book into the hotel until tomorrow when Burton would arrive to explain the next part of the plan.

All went smoothly for the family although there were a lot of questions being asked about what Burton and the boys were doing.

No one could answer these questions and even guessing was not helpful so Marion had called a halt to the queries by saying, "Enough, thank you, all will be revealed in the morning."

Even as she said these fateful words she felt a sharp twinge under her ribs. The baby was on the move too and seemed to want a part of the action.

Burton had given his instructions to Burt without expecting any comment. "Burt you are to ride to the thickest bush area near the creek. Here you are to light a hot fire with plenty of coals. You will take this branding iron I have been making over the past months and you will heat it until it is white hot. You will take two buckets and fill these with water. We will use these to dowse the fire when we are finished."

He turned to Ginger and explained his part in the plan. "Ginger, I want you to ride to Miss Becky's and arrange for us to have plenty of room in the barn at the back to hold some cattle and pigs. Tell Miss Becky that you are helping me out in readiness for the sales tomorrow morning. The little she knows the better."

He stopped talking to catch his breath and then

addressed both of them, "We have worked hard to get to this position and Mr Sirrat agreed that we were owed a lot of money for all the improvements and the way we have managed the farm. I am not prepared to just be kicked off and left with nothing by the greedy Sirrats. We are going to take the heifers and the pigs that have not been branded and we are going to put the BBJ brand on them. The Sirrats will be none the wiser as they have never been on the property to know what is here. We will then take them into Miss Becky's to tether them over night. At five in the morning we will all go and get the animals and walk them to the wharf and onto a ship bound for the north. Hopefully we can get one going all the way to the Daintree."

He paused in his speech and looked at the two boys.

Burt was young but had a wise head and was eager to fill his father's plan.

Ginger was almost a man and keen also but there passed a shadow across his face. He said nothing about what was concerning him, instead he rushed off for his horse and went careering through the back paddocks headed for the main road.

"Oh I almost forgot," said Burton to Burt, "You will need to drive the heifers with you and tether them to the trees. Take plenty of rope. Go."

Burton set off on his horse headed for town. Although he rode the stallion with some vigour he knew he would not catch Ginger.

He was well aware of the boy's background a part of which was as a handy horseman.

He reached the Rockhampton Wharf at 4pm and saw immediately that there were five ships at anchor.

He tethered his horse and briskly began moving from one ship to the next asking if they were sailing north.

He received an affirmative answer from the third ship but was disappointed to hear that they were about to sail on the evening tide.

He was directed to the Cirrus the fifth ship which according to the man speaking was due to leave at first light for Cairns. He thanked the man for the information and hurried off to see if it was correct.

The captain of the Cirrus was standing on the deck watching cargo being loaded and puffing on a pipe.

"Ahoy there," called Burton. "I'm told your sailing for Cairns first light."

"Aye," came the reply.

"Can you take three adults and five children as pay-ing passengers? All are well behaved."

The captain's interest was in the former part of the information because he was running low on cash and goods at the moment. Any extra dollars would be most welcome.

"Aye'" he again agreed. "Be a pound for the biggies and 20 pence for the wee ones making it £3/10 all up.

Burton eagerly reached for his wallet, extracted £4

and called, "You are a sight for sore eyes sir, here keep the change."

All the while he was talking he moved onto the gang plank and towards the captain. "Oh by the way we'll have some animals to take with us. There are six heifers and six piglets."

"That'll be easy," said the captain and he pointed to the stern where several pens had been erected and four crates used for moving pigs and chooks. "That'll be £2 more."

Burton nodded and added the extra money to the notes he was proffering.

"Much obliged, sir, and we'll see you and the others at first light. We sail at 6 no sooner, no later," said the captain.

Burton had accomplished the first part of the plan. He wondered how the others were going.

He rode hard back along the main road and as he topped a rise he saw Marion and the children in the buckboard.

He reined in and moved into the bush out of sight.

He heard them go by and after a few minutes spurred the horse towards the Cassowary homestead.

Ginger had made it to Miss Becky's in record time and made all the arrangements as requested by Burton.

He moved everything out of the barn until he had a spare space of 4 yards by 4 yards.

He took some rope and cut pieces about six feet long. These he tied to posts that held the barn up. He had ten ropes altogether and hoped that this would be enough.

He went inside and spoke to Miss Becky telling her that he would be away for the night but would need the barn for a little job.

She didn't mind and anyway she had learnt to trust him.

Burt in the meantime had rounded up the heifers and one of the bulls and herded them to the thick bush area near the creek. Here he slowed them down and with considerable patience and skill managed to lasso each and tie them to a tree.

The bull proved to be a tougher task as it would not allow itself to be roped. Every time Burt got into a position and threw the rope the cunning bull would toss its head and the rope would slither off onto the ground.

Eventually he decided to give up and wait for his father and Ginger to arrive.

Any way dad had not mentioned the bull so he might actually get into trouble for disobeying.

The reason he had brought the bull was twofold. It was the best bred bull in the district and worth a lot of money. Second reason was that he had noticed the branding was a lot like the BBJ that they were going to use on the heifers. He reasoned that if the brand was applied exactly over the other no one would be the wiser.

He began to collect firewood and dry grass to make the hottest fire he could. He bundled these all up and struck a match. The dry grass ignited instantly and it wasn't long before he was searching for larger pieces of wood to keep the inferno going

Half an hour later he had the white hot coals he wanted and so he fetched the branding iron and settled it into the centre of the fire.

It was getting dark when Burt heard the noise. It sounded like a pig squealing and he was a little afraid thinking it might be one of a herd of wild pigs coming out of the forested area.

These feral pigs could cause a lot of damage to farms and even humans if they antagonised them in any way.

The squealing got louder and closer.

Burt was sure he could count over five pigs as they all seemed to have a different squeal.

He found a stout stick to use as a weapon then changed his thinking. He grabbed a piece of rope and some dry grass. He tied the grass onto the end of the stick and shoved this into the fire. It lit and blazed brightly. He lifted the stick out of the fire and held it aloft like a torch.

A voice hailed from the darkness, "That's a great idea my boy a torch to show us the way."

Two riders burst out of the bush into the circle of

light thrown by the fire and the burning torch.

Tied to their saddles were a number of squealing pigs.

Burton and Ginger had arrived.

Burton was quick to notice the bull and said, "We're not taking the bull. It will be too much trouble, besides we already have its breeding in the heifers."

Everything else in the plan went smoothly and the trio arrived at Miss Becky's at four ten the next morning.

Burton had detailed what he had accomplished.

He asked Ginger to report his work followed by Burt.

The plan was going beautifully and by six the whole family would be safely on the Cirrus and headed for Cairns with <u>THEIR</u> cattle and pigs.

Left field was about to throw a curve ball and none of the men would see it coming.

Chapter 27

Madeline had made everyone comfortable and she was ready to settle down for the night.

Her mother had been so proud of the way she had taken the lead and got all the children working as one. Even little Keith had joined in and helped by carry light things to the buckboard and later into the hotel.

They had deliberately travelled light knowing that when they got to their final destination they would find all the clothing and furniture that they needed.

Meals could be picked up on the way or if things got tight there was always plenty of fruit like paw paws, pineapples, mangoes and other tropical fruit along the tracks.

A good cutting of cane sugar would last as a treat for many hours.

Water was plentiful in the pristine creeks that flowed out of the mountains in every direction.

It certainly had the feel of being God's Country.

In the morning they had to be awake and ready to move by five so Madeline had banged her head on her pillow five times to ensure she had set her internal alarm clock. Odd as it might seem she had been using this method all of her life and it had not failed her.

Left field threw its curve ball and it went swishing through to the keeper…

Marion awoke.

The pains in her tummy were stronger than usual and they lingered on and on.

She moved into a new position but that didn't help.

She felt a spasm a sure sign that the baby had decided it was time to come.

Marion was certain that she had the right dates. The little mischief maker was not due for another six weeks.

She began to breathe with quick intakes, just as the nurses had taught her during previous births.

This helped a bit but then a stronger spasm shook her resolve. She involuntarily called out.

Instantly Eva woke up and asked in the dark, "Are you alright mum?"

Marion whispered back, trying not to wake anyone else, "No I think the baby is coming."

Eva flew out of bed and turned on the electric light. Her movement and the bright light woke everyone except Madeline.

"What's going on?" asked Isobel sleepily.

Eva took charge, "Mama thinks the baby is coming so Isobel get your night gown on and fetch Mrs Jones and tell her that mum is having the baby. Ask her to call the ambulance."

Isobel grabbed her night gown and as she pulled it on she ran for the door.

Eva continued as leader, "Wake up Madeline."

Marion was still panting and trying to get her spasms under control but it was not working.

"Oh what will Burton think if I'm not here in the morning?"

"Don't worry about that," said Madeline as she came instantly awake from a dig in the ribs. "We'll get you and Eva to the hospital and you will stay there until the baby is born. Eva can find a place to board nearby. In the meantime we'll fulfil dad's wishes and then he can work out the rest of the plan."

When Burton turned up at the hotel next morning he was shocked and pleased to hear the Marion had been taken to hospital.

Madeline filled him in on the night's happenings and then outlined what they had decided to do.

"Good girl," praised Burton, "I couldn't have thought that through as well as you have. Has Eva got enough money for her board and to pay hospital bills?"

"Yes dad, mum gave her £20 this morning and then gave her purse to me. Here you can take it and look after it."

Madeline handed the dark green purse to her father and awaited his instructions.

"Right," began Burton. "The plan will change only slightly because your mum has gone off on her holiday."

Madeline smiled because it had always been the same when mum had another baby. "Dad referred to it as mum having a holiday. If only he knew what she had to go through and the pain she had to endure he would change his thinking."

"You are all to gather your things and take them downstairs. A delivery boy will take these to the wharf and have them loaded on to a ship called the Cirrus. We will go for a brisk walk out to see Miss Becky and Ginger."

At the mention of the name Ginger Madeline's eyes flickered but she remained quiet listening to Burton's instructions.

"So what are we waiting for let's go, the ship sails at six so we had best shake a leg or two."

At Miss Becky's all was quiet and in darkness.

Ginger was in the barn where six cattle and six piglets were tied up to poles.

He strained through the darkness trying to make out any figures that might be lurking around. He expected seven people to turn up any second.

"Of course he was feeling disconsolate rather than happy because he was about to part company with the truest family he had ever had the privilege knowing.

They were about to take the animals and march them onto a ship. They would sail away and he would never see them again.

This was living the nightmare over again.

In England where he had been born to a single

mother he had found himself abandoned in the poor house at the age of five.

He remembered nothing of his mother.

Ginger lived in an orphanage for seven years before being indentured to old Mr Frisworth, a local farmer.

He was a kindly man but frail and aging.

He was wonderful company and gave Ginger so much to look forward to. He would talk about the future and hoped Ginger would find the family he craved. Ginger had toiled away with his farm chores and learnt from Mr Frisworth how to ride a horse, plough fields with a one farrow plough and how to use a scythe to cut the hay.

By the time he was fifteen he was a handy farmer's labourer. He approached Mr Frisworth asking him to let him go on a journey to Brisbane Australia. He had read about Brisbane as the Queensland government was seeking farmer's labourers for their expanding agriculture industry. The old man acquiesced and that meant he was on his way to a new land and a new life.

In the gloom he started to make out movement near the front of the house.

The family had arrived so Ginger lit the hurricane lantern and the wick burnt dully. He flicked the glass into place and there was a fizzing noise as the kerosene was sucked up into the wick causing the flame to burn brightly. He waved the lantern and saw a similar signal returned.

As each child came through the barn doorway Ginger handed them a rope and whispered, "You have one of the heifers to lead to the ship. Hold tight and just walk with the rest of us."

He ignored Keith as he was too small and wouldn't be able to hold onto a frisky calf never mind a growing heifer.

Ginger handed Burton a rope and then puzzled asked, "Where's Eva and Marion?"

"Major disaster I'm afraid," said Burton, "Marion's been taken to hospital as the baby has decided to come. I've sent Eva with her so we are shorthanded and behind time. I want you to stay behind, wake Miss Becky and explain about Marion. Only tell her that Marion is in hospital and Eva needs somewhere to stay. Ask her to go to the hospital in the morning and make arrangements to help Marion and Eva. Give her this £10 note for her troubles. After you speak to her I want you to follow us to the wharf on the double with the other heifer."

Even as he was speaking Burton was tying a piglet onto each heifer so that where the cow went the pig would have to follow or be dragged along.

Everyone moved at Burton's whispered command.

Ginger ran for the back door to tell Miss Becky the news and to leave Burton's instructions with her.

She was a lovable old lady and very reliable.

After getting Miss Becky's guarantee that she could

handle her part in the plan Ginger turned to rush away.

Miss Becky called to him to wait. She walked over to him and gave him a hug and a light kiss on his cheek. Prophetically she said, "Take care and never forget me because I won't forget you."

"I'll be back in time for breakfast, you'll see."

The Rockhampton Wharf was busier than they had ever seen. All the ships' crews stopped work and pointed to the odd parade of children and one tall adult male leading a heifer and squealing behind were two piglets. The man also held tightly to the hand of a small boy.

Behind the man were three children with a heifer and two piglets. At the end of the parade was one young girl with long plaits towing a heifer and one piglet.

It was a sight for sore eyes as they would say in the retelling over the many years ahead.

The children and Burton continued along the wharf headed directly for the Cirrus.

The captain stood at the wheel and hailed the family. "Just in time there we are about to cast off."

"I've one more to come can you heave to a while?" Burton called back.

"No sir, cannot do. I made it plain yesterday that we would cast off at six sharp.

He glanced at his watch and loudly addressed the men standing on the wharf. "Cast off aft." The man at the stern untied the thick rope and tossed it onto the deck of the Cirrus.

The ship swung stern first out into the river.

All the while Burton had guided the children and all the animals to the holding pens. He was busily loading the piglets into the crates.

"Cast off forward," shouted the captain and the ship began to move slowly away from the wharf.

Chapter 28

As it sidled away a shout went up from way along the wharf and Ginger came sprinting around the corner.

He was yelling, "Wait up, wait up the Cirrus."

Behind him galloped a heifer and a piglet.

The entire wharf was soon in an uproar as man after man joined in the chorus, "Wait up the Cirrus!"

Others added other messages all bound for the captain's ears.

Others again began urging the flaming redheaded lad to run faster.

Ginger got to within 40 yards of where the Cirrus was slowly drifting into deeper water and he suddenly swerved to his left.

Years later he would tell all who would listen that he had made a calculated decision. To those on the jetty and on the Cirrus it seemed more like a stupid way to acknowledge that he'd missed the ship.

Ginger plunged into the river dragging the heifer and piglet with him.

He struck out for the middle of the river hoping that the Cirrus would come along side. The heifer was lowing and thrashing behind and the poor little piglet was being kicked and knocked under the water.

Miraculously Ginger reached the side of the Cirrus as she began to move down the river.

A roped net had been hung over the side by a quick thinking crew member and Burton and several others lined the area urging Ginger to grab onto the net. He was able to do so and was hauled, soaking wet onto the deck.

The heifer followed as four men grabbed it and heaved.

The piglet was easier to take on board but sadly it had drowned in all the confusion in the water.

The family was grateful to have Ginger back and safe but were saddened by the fate of the piglet. The ship's cook was rather pleased.

Burton put his arms around Ginger and took him below where he was towelled dry and dressed in warm clothes.

"Well it looks like you will have to be one of the family now, there's no way of turning back."

Ginger was so delighted at this suggestion that he threw his arms around Burton and hugged him tightly. He began to sob saying, "I've never had a real family, thank you, thank you from the bottom of my heart."

"Twas nearly the bottom of the river, whatever possessed you to make a dive for the ship?" asked Burton.

"Maybe I had a premonition that I would end up in the best family in the world. All I had to do was take a chance."

Burton and the family with their new brother George laid low in Cairns for over a month.

To survive and to keep out the boredom they did odd labouring jobs. Picking pineapples was a favourite but cane cutting was a definite to avoid at all costs. It was back breaking and the sharp leaves left little cuts all over your body. Often you would chance upon a snake. The deadly taipan was no stranger to this area and to cane fields.

On the 4th June, 1926 Max Johnson was born.

Actually he was named Max Johns and was born to Mrs Johns in Ward 7 of the Rockhampton District Hospital. The alias was being used by Marion and Eva so as to avoid the Sirrat family locating them.

After all the days Marion had been in hospital it would seem unlikely that the Sirrats had discovered that there were some cattle and pigs missing from their brother's farm.

Marion, Eva and baby Max said their goodbyes to Miss Becky a fortnight after the birth and sailed for Cairns.

The family was re-united two days later.

After lots of hugs, kisses and oh ahs over the baby, Burton made the announcement that they had all waited for, "Next stop is a quick one at Port Douglas and then we catch the ferry to the Daintree."

Chapter 29

The captain of the ferry Daintree was Chas Osborne. A jolly fellow with greying hair that peeped out behind a well-worn white cap. He wore white shirt and trousers and considered himself one of the best navigators in Queensland. He loved talking and he loved children, having four of his own.

As the Johnson family piled onto the Daintree Captain Osborne greeted each in turn and welcomed them aboard.

He even cooed over baby Max much to Marion's delight.

He asked Burton what he planned to do in the Daintree.

Burton outlined his ambitions and quoted from the newspaper clipping regarding Lucas-Hughes and the Australian Agricultural Group.

"You're in luck, Mr Johnson," said Captain Osborne, "Mr Hughes is booked on this ferry. He's due shortly with his manager as they are going up the river to check on progress of the dairy farms and the butter factory they have so far established."

Burton couldn't believe what he had just heard.

He had hunted in every town he had been in for

news of Mr Lucas-Hughes but nothing.

People always recalled when they'd last seen him.

Often the comment was, "Oh bad timing he was here a few days, weeks ago you've just missed him."

"When will he be back?"

"Sorry, not a clue."

Now here he was about to walk down the gangplank and spend a couple of hours on the same boat – incredible.

Lucas-Hughes was a formidable man more for the energy he sustained than for his physical statue. He was tall standing over the six foot mark by a touch.

He wore clothing befitting a man with riches.

He spoke with confidence on any subject thrown up. He was widely read and knew his businesses inside out. Nothing passed him without a full awareness.

He was a problem solver and a doer.

He would ride around his properties, breeze into towns and check on industries he owned all the while making decisions and directing his workers.

As he came down the gangway of the Daintree Burton was impressed and immediately introduced himself. He cut to the chase by saying, "Burton Johnson, sir, your newest dairy farmer on the Daintree River."

"Good to make your acquaintance, I've been looking forward to this moment. Your reputation and persistence precedes you by many months."

Burton was taken aback by this comment until he

realised that all his enquiries about Lucas-Hughes would have been relayed down the line to the entrepreneur by all the people Burton had spoken to.

Lucas-Hughes took an instant liking to this sun tanned gentleman from the south. He enjoyed the company of his wife, Marion and adored the children all of whom proved to be well behaved and well mannered.

While everyone was getting to know everyone else on the ferry, Daintree, Captain Osborne began barking orders. "Cast off, fore and aft we are on our way ladies and gentleman and children," he said this like a ringmaster at a circus.

The Daintree slid out of port and headed due east. The children lined the railing and watched the scenery pass by. After 20 minutes sailing Captain swung the wheel and the ship headed north. Away to the west the passengers could see mountains rising high into the sky. Some had fluffy white clouds hanging over them.

Captain Osborne approached Marion and said, "Begging your pardon missus but do you mind if I take your little ones to the bow and show them the environment as we move up the Daintree River? It can be a pretty foreboding place for first timers and especially children."

"Certainly Captain Osborne it would be a pleasure to allow you to help us out so willingly. If you don't mind I think my husband and I will join you."

The ship made a left turn and began moving northwest when Captain Osborne called out, "All Johnsons to the bow please Captain wants to address you all."

The children scamped forward and took up seats at the front of the ship. The sea was getting calmer as they made their way towards land. They could see ahead of them a break in the land that at first sight appeared to be a deep bay.

"Hi my hearties," said Captain Osborne, "What you see ahead of us is the mouth of the Daintree River and it is about to devour us all." At this joke he laughed heartedly and all the children giggled at his antics. "I want to tell you all I know about the Daintree River so that you will know what you might be facing in the next few months."

The ship kept chugging along and was moving across an unseen channel. The young lad at the helm seemed to be in his element as he made slight adjustments to the course so as to stay in the deeper water.

"Under us at the moment is about six fathoms of water and as we near the river that will drop to four," explained Captain Osborne. "The river is quite deep mainly because it gets scoured out every year by flash flooding. These floods can be very dangerous and I'll tell you more about them as we get nearer to the Village."

"Village?" queried Madeline.

"Yes we have a lovely little village about 16 miles upstream and that's where we are headed. There's a jetty to pull up to and shops, butter factory, timber mill and some houses. Oh I almost forgot there's a school as well."

There was a mixed response to the last comment with Eva and Isobel showing delight whereas Keith pulled a face and then put his head down. The two older children Madeline and Burt showed indifference as they were nearly past primary school age. Max let out a squawk and then settled to happily feed from Marion who had discretely moved to the far side of the boat away from the group but within earshot.

Captain Osborne ignored the responses he noted from the children at the mention of a school. As a child himself he wasn't keen and ended up on the farm helping out at the age of twelve.

He pointed with his suntanned, hairy right arm towards an island that was to the starboard side of the boat and explained, "That's Snapper Island. The land that juts out towards the island is called Point Tribulation and was named by Captain Cook when he sailed this way on his way around the World. The beautiful white sandy beach is where we bring everyone from the Daintree for an annual picnic. Lots of fun and plenty to explore so Mrs Johnson put that on your social calendar." He looked towards Marion who nodded and then realised why she had moved to the other side.

He quickly turned back to his captive audience and continued, "If you look behind us you will see the

Pacific Ocean. This is to the east. Who can tell me what rises in the east in the morning?"

Eva was the clever one when it came to general knowledge, mainly because she loved to read anything she could get her hands on, and she answered immediately, "The Sun!"

"Correct," said Mr Osborne, "So we now know one of the directions. The sun sets in the west and that is the direction we are moving. As you can see ahead there are lots of mountains. So when you are working out your bearings ocean is to the east and mountains to the west. The really high mountain almost straight ahead is Mount Alexandra."

"It's like Mount Warning from back at Bray's Creek where we come from," said Madeline. "Is it a plug of an ancient super volcano?"

"Don't think so," replied Mr Osborne, "But we did have volcanoes in this area millions of years ago. Now where was I, oh yes, if you look towards the shore of the river you will see a tangle of tree trunks with long rope like roots all sitting in the water. These are mangrove and are impossible to find your way through. There are also lots of creatures that can hurt you so we don't venture into these at any time."

At this point Mr Osborne looked back at the wheel house and indicated for the boat to be taken towards the shore on the port side.

"Now I'm going to show you something you must

be very careful of. In our rivers and creeks we have huge saltwater crocodiles. They are very dangerous and have been known to kill people. Now I know that will alarm you but the Daintree is not for the faint-hearted and as you will be staying a while you need to know all the dangers and how to keep yourself safe. This morning I observed one of our biggest crocodiles sunbathing on the beach just ahead. I want you to look very closely and tell me when you can see it."

The boat slowed as it edged towards the brownish black mud that was the beach. Overhanging vegetation and fallen trees made it difficult to see into the undergrowth. All eyes strained towards the beach but no one said a word.

The boat ran parallel to the river's edge which was about six yards away. Still nothing even though they had covered some thirty yards since Mr Osborne had asked them to find the crocodile. He raised his arm and the boat engine cut out and they sank into the dark water. Mr Osborne reached into a small hessian bag that lay at his feet and pulled out a white feathered chicken that was dead. He held it above his head and moved it back and forth.

"Now I want you to see what you will be dealing with. Please stay nice and quiet and calm as you can't be hurt while you are in the boat."

Chapter 30

Captain Osborne tossed the chicken towards the muddy beach. It landed with a splash one yard short.

At the same time a huge, chunky log some 20 feet in length that was lying against the bank came to life and with lightning speed crashed into the water.

Plumes of water and mud went flying into the air and two jaws opened and snapped shut over the floating chicken carcass.

Everyone jumped backwards away from the beast and its gaping mouth.

Isobel and Keith let out a scream and grabbed at their father's trousers for comfort and safety.

The huge monster paused with the chicken visible in its jaws. It flicked its head upwards and let go of the morsel it had in its mouth.

The chicken flew through the air turning end over end. Feathers scattered from the corpse as it reached its zenith. It seemed to pause for a split second before turning end over end back down.

The crocodile waited patiently for the headless chicken to descend. It lifted its head so that everyone could see it was half out of the water. The jaws opened and the chicken plummeted in. With a swallow the chicken was devoured. The crocodile slid back into the water and disappeared under the ferry.

"That ladies and gentleman is Scarface, one of the largest saltwater crocodiles in the Daintree River.

"And that ladies and gentlemen is an example of how well they can camouflage themselves against the river bank.

"They have lightning speed and their jaws clamp over a victim like a steel bear trap. They have rows of sharp round teeth and once they take a prey they don't let go until it is dead.

"Small animals such as the chicken they will chew and swallow. Large ones like cattle or pigs they take into the water and roll over and over. This is called the death roll, it drowns the catch."

All the children and even Marion and Burton were visibly shocked by what they had just witnessed.

Burton was about to chastise Mr Osborne for being so callous with his children's well-being.

As he tried to decide on the right words to use and the tone of voice that would be appropriate it dawned that the crocodile lesson was imperative to the safety of each and every one of them in the family.

He kept his silence.

Mr Osborne had not finished with the crocodiles just yet.

"We'll idle up a bit and I'll show you one so that

you get a good understanding of what they look like. I would dare to suggest the old Scarface was a bit too quick for you all to get a clear look."

He gestured to the helmsman who edged the boat forward but keeping a good ten yards from the shore. "There we are. Who will see the new crocodile first?" challenged Mr Osborne.

He was pointing towards a wider beach than the previous one but it was still a jumble of branches, logs, leaves and muddy swirls.

"There it is!" shouted Ginger, "Next to the log that has a V shaped branch sticking upwards."

"Well spotted lad," said Mr Osborne and then continued his lesson. "This is a female so she will be smaller than the old bull we just encountered. Look at her colours that include black, brown, grey and olive – all the colours that let her blend into the muddy bank and the blackness of the river water.

She is just as nasty and just as quick especially at mating time and when the eggs are being hatched out. Mating is during October and November, and they nest in December through to April.

The nest is a mound usually on the river or creek banks and is made of vegetation and soil.

She lays 40 to 70 eggs and covers them with the rotting vegetation. It is important for her to have the nest above the flood level as the little crocodile in the egg, called the embryo will drown. You see they breathe through the shell. After about 90 days they hatch out and stay close to their mother as she will protect them. They have a high pitch squawking call to let her know if they are in danger or if they wish to attract her attention. Take a good look so that when you see one you will know to stay well clear. If they are in the water you won't see much at all, possibly a ripple on the water if they're moving or the tops of their eyes. Always check ever so carefully before you cross the shallows or if you go swimming."

At the conclusion of the crocodile session Mr Osborne gave a swirling arm movement and the engine picked up its revs and the boat surged forward.

"I'll be back in a little while so please enjoy the scenery. I hope I haven't upset or scared anyone too much." With that he walked off towards the wheel house.

Twenty minutes passed like hours as the boat chugged its way along the river.

The children excitedly pointed out different objects that they thought they recognised from their knowledge of the scrub back at Bray's Creek and their trek along the coast of Queensland.

Captain Osborne arrived back and immediately signalled to the young man at the helm to turn right or starboard. The boat responded to the rudder adjustment and it made a beeline for the mangrove lined shore.

"You have probably noted that there are only a few farmers living along the river. In fact there are only three and they are a little way back. If you live too close to the bank you have the crocodile problem and the floods. Floods are common in the wet season, December to about April and some can reach ten or more feet. Ah, here's what I want to show you all."

Again a signal but this time it was to stop the engine.

The boat slowed markedly as the propellers stopped turning.

The boat eased towards the shore and then lined up parallel to the high muddy banks.

Everyone strained to see if there was another crocodile lurking in the shallows.

Keith moved back from the railing and reached out for his father's hand.

"Now," began Mr Osborne, "I have shown you the most dangerous creature on the Daintree so let's talk about another reptile that is more deadly than his mate the crocodile. I suppose you know what a reptile is and what characteristics the family has."

He looked around at the mix of nods and head shakes and ploughed on with his talk. "Reptiles all have scales and lay eggs. If you want a big word to use then say they are ectothermic which means they can make their body temperature vary from the outside temperature. The types of reptiles include turtles, lizards, snakes and crocodiles. The reptile group I'm about to show you and warn you about is the snake family. I'm sure you know a little already but here in the Daintree we have some of the most poisonous snakes in the world. Not only are they deadly but they live in the oddest of places. Has anyone spied the snake yet?"

With this challenge everyone looked at the bank but there was nothing but mangrove.

Snakes to most people lived on the ground where they slithered here and there at a terrific speed. There was nowhere on the bank for the creatures to live.

"If you all follow my pointing you will see that you have to look upwards and back beyond the mangroves. About four yards away from the edge of the water the forest or scrub starts. Here trees and undergrowth of all types grow. If you look carefully at the tall tree in front of us you will see what looks like a branch, about 20 feet up. That is an Amethystine or Scrub Python about twenty feet long. He lays up there soaking up the sun. He is harmless but never trust any snake because many aren't."

The children finally spotted the gigantic snake and there were lots of questions being thrown back and forth.

"Whoa," said Mr Osborne, "Let's see if I can at least answer a few of the queries I just heard. The deadliest is the Taipan which grows to eight feet, is dark brown to light straw in colour. It lives on the ground and loves to eat mice and rats. It will happily live in your barn or even the house if you let the vermin multiply. The Eastern Brown Snake is a dark tan with a creamy belly. The Death Adder is short and squat with banded shades of grey and brown. The Adder grows to three feet and has long fangs. Finally the Red-Bellied Black Snake has a glossy black back and its undercarriage is pink to red."

"No mice mum, make sure we don't have any in the house ever!" pleaded Isobel.

She had let her vivid imagination run wild imagining a twelve foot taipan slithering up the bedpost, under the blankets and then seeking out her creamy bare leg. Or maybe it was the mouse that had run under the blankets and the taipan was in full flight after it only to come upon a larger more delicious morsel.

"Now, quieten down," said Mr Osborne, "It is unlikely that anyone of you will ever see a snake while you are in the Daintree. Very few of our farmers or their families have come across these creatures. I'm trying to impress upon you the probabilities and what could harm you if you aren't vigilant. The most important part of this talk is to ask you all to tell me what you would do if you or anyone you were with got bitten by a snake."

Ginger's right hand shot up and before he was asked he began to tell all in earshot of what he would do to help a snake bite victim.

"I would try to see what type of snake it was and make sure it went away. I would find something to act as a tourniquet. I would find the fang mark and come above the next joint and tie the tourniquet tightly there. I would then make a loop and put a stick in the loop so I could turn the stick and this would tighten the tourniquet even more and stop the poison going to the heart. I would then help the victim home or if there were others with me I would send them for help. If I had a sharp knife or something I would cut through the fang marks to make it bleed and then suck out the blood and poison. I would spit the blood out making sure I didn't swallow any."

Mr Osborne had put his hand up to stop Ginger at various points along the speech but Ginger ploughed on.

He had learnt all about snakes on his voyage out from England.

The First Mate had gathered a different group of passengers each evening to tell them about the hazards they would meet in Australia. He had arranged them in groups according to where they were going to disembark. Ginger had been in the Queensland group.

He had heard the First Mate talking about a taipan and the Red-bellied Snake. It was what to do if bitten, that had been fixed in his brain.

"Excellent, excellent my lad and spoken like a true teacher. If any of you need a refresher course just call up your big brother and he'll set you right," said Mr Osborne.

Burton was about to correct Mr Osborne and say, "The lad is not family he's an orphan from the Mother Country," when he bit his tongue.

Thinking about it for a little he decided that he needed to talk to Ginger and the family later when they got settled about an important issue. For now he would keep the topic under his hat.

Mr Osborne signalled to the wheelhouse and the motor started and the boat turned back into midstream and chugged onwards.

Burton walked over to Mr Osborne and thanked him profusely for his tips to the family.

"Do you do that for all the new ones into the Daintree?" he asked.

"Almost all if they are interested," said Mr Osborne. "Sometimes I find a family that becomes quite upset and refuse to listen to anything more. The chicken and crocodile stunt alarms some. Others get angry because they think you are belittling their knowledge although if truth be known they are quick to come around to my farm and ask me for information when they run afoul of the wildlife."

"You have my wife and my eternal gratitude, Mr Osborne, and I hope that you will allow us to call you friend throughout our stay."

"That sir I would be happy to oblige. By the way my name is Chas."

He held out his brawny right hand.

"Burton, and my wife is Marion," said Burton grasping the proffered hand in his and shaking firmly.

Marion smiled to herself as she watched the exchange between the two men.

She marvelled at how easily her husband made friends and knew he would be loyal to this Mr Osborne throughout their stay in the Daintree.

She was having a few second thoughts given the demonstrations that she and the family had just been through.

Maybe a few months like all the other times and Burton would get his wanderlust legs back again and they would move somewhere else safe.

Chapter 31

The boat trip up the far reaches of the river was one bend after another.

The ancient river had slowed over the millions of years that it had scoured through this country.

As it slowed it meandered and dropped its cargo of silt and vegetation. The silt built up on the slow sides resulting in lovely sandy beaches.

The river was also getting narrower.

Everyone jumped when the hooter sounded loud and clear. The first hoot was followed by another and another.

On the right side or starboard farms could be seen.

The flats were fenced and cows grazed contentedly.

Farm houses were built further back on the hill slopes or on top of the smaller hillocks.

Burt nudged Ginger and asked, "How many farms can you see?"

"My question would be how many farms are operating out here?" replied Ginger.

Another sweeping bend and again the hooter blasted out three times.

This time everyone expected the sudden noise and joined in making their own hoots.

Ahead Burt could make out a building on top of a hill. "What's that dad?" he called to his father who was still holding onto Keith's hand.

"That must be the Butter Factory, son," his father called back. "It is supposed to be on a high part of the river bank and has a saw mill close by. They use the same boiler to produce steam to drive all the engines."

"Correct, Burton," it was Mr Lucas- Hughes who had approached while all the hooting was happening. "That's where you will deliver your milk each morning and if you need any planks or fence posts the mill will cut these to your exact size."

"Sounds like you have everything under control out here," replied Burton.

"Yes but it all keeps me on the go, never a chance to rest unless you catch a boat."

"So," thought Burt, "that's why we haven't seen Mr Lucas-Hughes all trip, he's been below having a well-earned rest."

The diesel motor began to slow and the boat moved right, out towards the middle of the river.

From their advantage points on the railing at the bow the family could make out a jetty below what was now identified as the Butter Factory.

The helmsman brought the boat around in a sweeping circle so she pointed back the way she had come. He eased the boat towards the wooden planks of the jetty.

Captain Osborne ran forward and grabbed a

mooring rope. As the boat slowed he jumped onto the jetty and secured the line.

He was quite agile for a big man. He ran astern and tied the other mooring rope to the jetty.

He walked back to the centre of the wharf and called to the young lad on the wheel. "Cut the motor and help me secure the gangplank."

An instant later all was quiet. The constant 'thanka thanka' that they had put up with for nearly two hours was silenced.

The gangplank in place and all the passengers began to alight.

Mr Lucas-Hughes was first striding out and excusing himself to all and sundry. He was soon walking briskly up the steep embankment towards the Butter Factory.

Burton took the family and Ginger to the stern of the boat.

Here they began issuing orders so that the heifers and piglets were again roped together and allocated to each member of the family.

"I'm not staying behind and I'm not going swimming this time," said Ginger and everyone laughed remembering the episode back in Rockhampton all those days ago.

"Where are we going?" asked Marion as they finally had all disembarked.

"Follow me and we'll find out," said Burton and he set off.

The parade was followed by Marion, who was carrying little Max, followed by the girls and then Burt and Ginger brought up the rear. Keith still clung to his father's hand as no crocodile or taipan was going to get him.

Everyone stepped out as it was refreshing walking around after being on the ferry.

"There's a sport's ground over the rise to our right. Mr Lucas-Hughes told me about it when I was talking to him

"We tether the animals and then make our way up to the village of Daintree. There are a few shops up past the Butter Factory. We can get something to eat and drink.

"Mr Lucas-Hughes will then send his local manager to explain how we get our allotment and how to get there."

All the while he was talking the family continued to walk over the rise.

Before them they could see the oval and to one side was a small wooden shed with railing alongside used for tethering horses.

After tying up the heifers to the railing they made their way back towards the Butter Factory.

They followed a track that would take them to the left of the main building and here they found the terrain flattened out.

A number of shops and houses had been built on the flat ground, high above the flood level of the river.

One shop had a blackboard out the front shaped like a sandwich board. In white chalk a poorly spelt message invited them in for 'sand witches, cack and tee'.

As they entered a feminine voice called from out the back, "Be with you in a sec folks, just take a seat."

The owner of the voice soon appeared and greeted them one again before introducing herself. "I'm Annie Cockram owner and cook of Annie's Get Your Bun."

At this quip she laughed uproarishly and the family joined in. They weren't laughing at the pun which they missed but simply at Annie's laugh.

"Mr and Mrs Johnson and family," Burton began the introductions, "We've just arrived on the ferry and intend to stay a while on one of the dairy farms around here. Just call us Burton and Marion."

"Well nice to meet you at last we've been hearing about you all for the last year or two. It got to the stage where we decided that old Lucas-Hughes might have lost his marbles and made you all up. We were hoping that you were real because your large family will give the local school the boost in numbers it needs."

At the mention of school Isobel asked, "Where is the school?"

"Not so fast there missy," said Annie, "Need to know who you all are if you don't mind. We are going to be neighbours like so you be comin' into the shop for things it is nice to be able to say your names."

"That's a fair call," said Burton and he began at the oldest, "The ginger headed one is George but we call him Ginger, then there's Burt, Madeline here is the oldest girl followed by Eva and then Isobel. This one near me is Keith and the baby is Max."

Right on cue Max let out a bawl as if doing his own introduction and Marion was quick to ask, "Do you have a glass of milk, heated for the baby. I'm afraid I've run out and it would be better to give him the bottle in this public place."

Annie was only too pleased to oblige and bustled off to the kitchen.

She was in her forties, short and stout with greying hair. She had a ruddy complexion and little freckles under her eyes and across the bridge of her nose.

As one would expect of a chief cook and bottle washer and working alone she wore that look of near exhaustion.

She had already served some twenty lunches to the itinerants that came and went in the Daintree.

She turned her left arm upwards and trickled a tiny droplet of the milk she had in the glass onto the wrist. "As Goldilocks would have said, 'Not too hot and not too cold but just right'."

Again she set off everyone with her odd laughing as she handed the milk to Marion.

"Thank you so much," said Marion and she poured the fluffy white liquid into the baby bottle that she had produced from within the brown carry bag she always carried.

"Now what will the rest of you have?" she asked as she produced a HB pencil and a note book made from blank paper held together with a piece of binder twine. The string had been pulled through a hole at one end and then another at the other end before being pulled lightly together and tied with a bow.

Burton began ordering for everyone.

There was never any time for separate or special orders.

Everyone knew that they would all get the same and the only variation would be in the quantity.

Marion did not order as she waited patiently for everyone to finish and then ate leftovers. This saved money and was a way of leaving plates shiny clean. If she needed more Marion would then help herself or order as required.

"A round of ham sandwiches for each and a small glass of lemonade," said Burton. "Marion will happily wait and may order after she has fed the baby."

That was a diplomatic way of explaining the tradition that had been built up between himself and Marion regarding the eating arrangements.

"That makes, let me see… 1, 2, 3, 4, 5, 6, 7 rounds of ham sandwiches and seven glasses of lemonade. Be ready in a jiffy."

There was little conversation at the table as the family waited for their meal.

At one point Madeline asked quietly, "Where are we staying tonight dad?"

Burton thought for a moment and addressed everyone with his reply, "Shortly we are to meet a Mr Morrish who is Mr Lucas-Hughes' manager here in the Daintree. He will explain to us all what the arrangements he has made. Until then let's all enjoy our meal and then we'll go for a walk around the town."

The sandwiches soon arrived and distributed to each.

The lemonade came in small glasses that looked very much like used vegemite jars washed and ready for use.

Everyone was so peckish as they had not eaten since 6 this morning and now the sun was well past its zenith.

The sandwiches were surprisingly scrumptious and the bread was fresh and tasty.

The lemonade bubbled and fizzed showing it had come from a newly opened bottle.

After eating Burton suggested everyone wait out on the verandah so that Marion could finish feeding Max and herself.

She was soon tucking into half a sandwich left by Keith and some crusts neglected by both Eva and Isobel.

How many times she had told those girls they wouldn't have curls if they didn't eat their crusts she couldn't remember.

"Had enough, love or do you want me to order more?" asked Burton.

"No I'm fine but a drink of milk would go down nicely."

"Excuse me Annie," called Burton.

In an instant Annie flew out of the kitchen, pencil in hand and notebook ready. "Yes Mr Johnson, what else might you like?"

"The meal was lovely and the lemonade so refreshing. Could we bother you for a large glass of milk for my wife?"

"No bother at all," replied Annie as she set off at a frenetic pace to do their bidding. For all the time they knew her she set this cracking pace and was always there to please.

Chapter 32

A stroll around the town showed that it was rather small, even smaller than Tyalgum back in Northern New South Wales where they hailed from. Well Bray's Creek to be precise but that location was not a town only an area.

There was a lodging house of two storeys built of local timber, a butcher's shop with sausages hanging from hooks in the window and trays of red meat on the bench behind the glass. Three plucked chickens and a plucked duck lay on some sawdust.

"Looks neat and tidy," commented Burton, "We may need to use that until we settle in."

Next was a co-op, a store that had everything and if they didn't have it the proprietor was always ready to order it in. They didn't enter but stood outside looking through the door and at the window display.

Further on was a house that someone lived in. They knew because there was washing on a line out the back.

They left the main street where the shops were and headed left along a walking track.

In the distance they could see two buildings, one was larger than the other.

As they approached the smaller building it became

clear that it was a typical Queenslander house built on stilts to allow the breeze to blow through and thus cool the inside. It had steep steps at the front and the back.

A small well-worn path led from the back of the house to the second larger building.

A fence of wire strands encircled both buildings so it meant that they belonged to the same owner.

At the corner of the property that they were approaching they could make out a sign on a log. Someone had cut out one side to make the log flat and here they had engraved the words 'Daintree Village School No. 1027

"It's the school," whooped Isobel. She loved reading and learning and going to school to meet new friends.

She had missed this part of her life for the past three years.

The last school she went to was the one run by her grandmother, Mary Jane. She used to combine an education with Sunday school. Nevertheless all the local children who attended learnt lots of things.

Eva was also excited as she loved to go to school because it gave her lots of people to socialise with. Her main aim in life as she moved towards her teens was to be able to converse with others who had had experiences unlike anything she had had.

No one seemed to be about so it must have been after 3.30pm, the usual time schools in Queensland closed for the day.

The family continued on and found themselves moving in a sweeping arc through heavy tropical growth. Eventually they came out on the other side of the school.

Here they could see a gigantic tree with numerous branches coming off at all angles growing just inside the school fence.

"That's a funny looking tree," said Burt, "I wonder what it is?"

Everyone was standing against the fence looking up towards the top of the tree. Sparsely covered in leaves it towered over a hundred feet.

The family's attention was next caught by the sound of galloping hoofs.

A rider came from the direction of the town and reined up in front of Burton.

"Mr Johnson, sir, I'm Charley Morrish, Mr Lucas-Hughes sent me to find you all."

"How do, Mr Morrish," replied Burton, "Good to make your acquaintance."

"Mr Lucas-Hughes wants me to get you settled in and then take you out to your farm. So first thing is to ask you to walk back to town and meet me outside the Lodging abode. Know where that is?"

"Yes sir we have made ourselves knowledgeable of some of the town so we'll catch up with you soon."

Mr Morrish turned his black steed and galloped away towards the shops.

"Seems everyone is in one mighty hurry around here," said Burton almost to himself.

The family set off to walk the 200 yards back to the village.

As they moved they could see the heifers and piglets away to their right. They were all lying down resting. The ferry trip had taken a fair bit out of them.

Mr Morrish was waiting outside the Lodge when the eight Johnsons and Ginger turned up.

"We are going to have to billet you all out for three or four days so these are the arrangements Mr Lucas-Hughes has put in place. He'd be mighty happy if you concur with his planning. Mrs Johnson and the three girls and the two youngest stay in the Lodge with full board, breakfast, lunch and dinner. The men will move the stock to the new farm and then stay at the Hayden's, who live next door, until we can make the house on your farm habitable. How does that sound?"

Burton as head of the family spoke for everyone, "That sure sounds like a sensible plan Mr Morrish. You please lead the way."

Mr Morrish took Marion and the others of her entourage into the lodge and within five minutes came back out and called to the men, "Right they are happily bedded down now let's get the animals you have to a place where they can be fed, watered and rested."

Burton followed Mr Morrish and although he was impressed that they knew a lot about them and what they had been doing he kept mum.

The cattle and pigs were taken back to the river and down onto a long sand bank.

The sand started from the jetty and extended some 60 yards downstream. Lying on the sand were five small rowboats, oars stored inside and each was tethered to the remnants of mangrove roots.

Further along was a larger boat with an out board motor attached.

Burton looked at the two boys and both shook their heads.

Even though no words were spoken it was clear what Burton was thinking, "Did you two notice the boats when we first arrived?"

Obviously from the shakes of the heads they did not. It was probably due to the course taken by the ferry as they swept into the centre of the river and turned in a tight circle.

All eyes were on the other bank and then the wheel house obscured their view until the Butter Factory and the jetty came into view.

Mr Morrish walked off towards the boat with the outboard motor leaving instructions for the three men to load the animals into the two nearest flatties.

"Flatties? What is he talking about dad?" queried Burt.

"The little rowboats son," his father replied, "They have a flat bottom and their draw in the water isn't much allowing rowers to paddle up shallow creeks."

Ginger managed to get one heifer and a piglet into a boat but the second was very reluctant.

Burton handed his ropes to Burt and picked up the heifer and with one heave landed it beside the first. "Tie then onto the rowlocks without any slack," ordered Burton to Ginger. He picked up another heifer and unceremoniously dumped this one in the front of the boat.

He untied the rope holding the boat from the mangrove roots and came back to push the boat into the river.

The heifers were well tied but still restless causing the boat to rock violently.

"I'll get thrown into the river if you lot don't settle," remonstrated Ginger. He began to soothe them and give each a pat on the nose. The piglets were easily loaded.

"Burt let's get these other three cows in boat number two. You get in and we'll try the same method."

This time everything went smoothly. It was as though the second lot of cows and piglets had taken note of what to do and that was it.

In the meantime Mr Morrish had started the outboard motor with two strong pulls on the starter cord. He moved the boat out from the shore and came chugging towards the two flatties.

"Mr Johnson can you wade out and take the ropes in the front of each flattie and carry them over to this boat."

Burton did as he was requested.

He climbed nimbly into the motor boat and held onto the two ropes. By holding his arms akimbo he was able to have one float along to the left and the other to the right and about three yards astern.

Mr Morrish called out, "We're away so keep a sharp look out. Mr Johnson let me know if we lose a flattie or the animals cause a problem. You are my spotter."

The boat gathered speed as Mr Morrish eased the accelerator handle forward. The outboard motor increased its revs and the two flatties moved along too.

They hugged the edge of the bank staying about five yards away from the entangled roots of the mangrove.

After about ten minutes the boat slowed and made a gentle left hand turn.

At first Burton thought they were going to smash into the mangrove and he was about to yell out a warning.

Luckily he noticed a break in the mangrove just in time and realised that they were heading for a new stream.

"This is Stewart Creek," called Mr Morrish without looking back.

He was busy guiding the boats along the much narrower waterway.

Every now and again he would steer the boat from one side to the other to avoid low hanging branches or logs that had fallen into the water. The denseness of the scrub almost blocked out the light and gave one the feeling of being lost in a jungle setting.

The boat was now barely idling along due to the numerous hazards that kept cropping up or jutting out.

After 20 minutes or thereabouts Burton noticed another stream flowing in from his right. It was narrower again than the Stewart but the flow seemed stronger.

"That's the Douglas Creek," shouted Mr Morrish, "Comes a long way from the mountains, flows all year round just like this one."

Finally they came out onto a wider section that had a sweeping sand bank on the right side. The sand extended for 50 yards and was about ten yards wide.

Mr Morrish headed for the bank and ran the boat up onto the sand. He jumped out and grabbed the rope that was attached to the front of the boat.

He ran to a large tree trunk that was lying on the sand and tied the rope on. This was how they anchored the boats on the Daintree.

Burton began hauling the flatties towards the stern of the boat. He called to the two boys to push the flatties onto the sand and wait for him.

He scrambled out of the boat and took charge of Ginger's flattie.

He soon had all the animals out and on dry land.

"Right," said Mr Morrish, "Take these cows up

to the barn you can make out about 150 yards away. Lock them in and make sure they have feed and water to last until tomorrow morning. You will find all you need."

Burton took his two heifers and began to walk towards the barn and the other two boys followed closely behind.

"When you've finished get back here and I'll take you along to the Hayden's place.

A little under half an hour later and a careful boat run up the very narrow Douglas Creek the trio was meeting Mr and Mrs Hayden.

Mr Morrish said his goodbyes and went back down the creek headed for the jetty and Mr Lucas-Hughes. He had to report that all was well with the plan and everyone was happily and comfortably settled in.

Chapter 33

Barry Hayden ushered the three visitors into his home and introduced them to his wife Sally.

She was hovering over a large pot of stew that was bubbling on the stove. "Honey the Johnsons have arrived," said Barry.

His dark haired wife turned and smiled at the new-comers. "Hello and welcome," she said brushing her curls from falling into her eyes, "I'm Sally. I'm sure you must be famished after such a long day. I hope you all like lamb stew."

Burton answered for the others, "That will do fine Sally. I'm Burton and these two are Burt and Ginger."

As he spoke he pointed to each boy in turn. They both nodded and smiled.

They sat down at the table that already was set with a pristine white table cloth covering the surface.

Each place was marked by the arrangements of sil-ver knives, forks and spoons and a bowl.

Sally lifted the pot of stew with her right hand and taking a ladle in her left began sharing out the meat and vegetables into each bowl.

"Much easier to serve stew in a bowl than a plate," she explained. "We like ours nice and watery so that we can dip the fresh bread in and soak it up."

The Haydens took up a chair apiece and the others settled into the spare chairs that were placed around the table.

Everyone agreed that it was scrumptious stew and commended Sally on her cooking.

The mound of bread and the lovely bright yellow butter soon disappeared as they all tucked in.

Burton hit it off with Barry Hayden and before long they were trading stories of how they ended up in the Daintree. Each had an epic to tell so the stories lasted well into the night.

Barry Hayden's story started back with his father. When he was a youngster they had been living in Sydney and doing quite well.

His father worked for the Post Master General's Office or the PMG. He was at first a postman delivering letters and parcels around the Rocks area.

As he became more experienced and senior he was given a number of promotions until he was offered the job as manager of the Post Office at the town of Bathurst. This was a busy town and relied very much on agriculture especially sheep.

His wife Dawn was reluctant at first to leave Sydney as she had established a family and a small group of friends.

They rented a comfortable house although the cost

was above what they could really afford if they wanted to save and do better in life.

Barry was thirteen when the move was announced and was quite excited as was his older brother Tom and his younger sister Tess.

He recalled seeing his mother in tears over the week after his dad had explained that he had the chance to run his own Post Office and that he would be doubling his wage.

They arrived in Bathurst on January 1st in the year 1905 and settled in.

Everything seemed fine to Barry and his siblings.

Dad set off to work each day and mum busied herself with the new house. The house was far larger and more comfortable than the one back in Sydney.

After two years of fun and excitement for the three children mum made the announcement that she was leaving and going back to Sydney.

She felt lonely, she missed her parents and no one in Bathurst wanted to be friends with her.

Barry, Tom and Tess were lined up and asked to declare who they wanted to live with, mum or dad.

It would appear that the parental argument had already been had and finished with, as this declaration was final.

Dad had obviously decided to stay with his job in Bathurst.

Barry had loved it in Bathurst and had a job as the postman for the eastern section of the city.

Riding a bicycle gave him a healthy lifestyle and he loved getting out into the suburbs and saying hello to all the folk he delivered letters to.

His dad was his boss and he loved to hear him say, "Barry one day you could be the Post Master General of the whole of New South Wales."

Barry felt immensely proud when he heard those words although there was some doubt that it would ever happen.

Barry was nearing his seventeenth birthday when his mother and two siblings caught the train back to Sydney.

He would never forget the scene as the steam engine let out a screeching toooooot and there was a billowing of steam then the huge iron wheels began to turn. Slowly at first and then it gained speed and sped off around the corner.

He could still see his mum's arm drooped out of the window but not waving.

Tom was hanging out the window waving crazily and Tess was sobbing into a handkerchief as she looked mournfully back.

Dad gave a sort of salute and Barry waved with both arms.

"Well it's just you and me now," said dad and he put his arm around Barry's shoulders and they walked off towards home.

Of course there was one thing that had really made Barry decide to stay. He had not told any of the others but he had met a delightful young lady called Sally Parker.

She lived out along one of the roads that he delivered mail to.

They bumped into each other one day when she ran down the path to collect the letters before he pushed them through the hole of the post box.

She was moving quite fast and had misjudged her attempt to get him to hand over the letters.

She cannoned into him and he fell from the bicycle landing heavily on the ground.

He had not even realised she was there he was so intent on placing the three letters in the box at number 62 and then checking the next house number of the bundle of mail he was still holding.

They both ended up in a tangle with the young lady apologising profusely. "Oh I'm so sorry, so sorry," she kept repeating.

Barry was about to give her a mouthful when he looked up and discovered he was staring at a beautiful, dark, curly haired young lady. Her hair was cropped short and she was slim and athletic. She was wearing a green, cotton blouse buttoned up at the front. A pair of dark green shorts complimented her blouse. She was barefooted. The only odd thing he noted was that she had light reddish rings around her hazel eyes and the marking was more pronounced in the corners and across the bridge of her nose.

"It's alright," Barry kept assuring her until finally he introduced himself.

"I'm Barry Hayden, at your service mam, one day to be the Post Master General of New South Wales!"

The young girl stopped her apologising and began laughing uncontrollably; in fact it got to the stage where Barry thought she would never be able to take a breath again.

She slowly controlled herself but still needed to take gulps of air, "I'm Sally Parker and I'm going to be Queen of England."

That set off the laughter once again.

Barry felt so embarrassed that he just sat and stared.

After a while he stood up, hauled his bicycle onto its two wheels and tried to compose himself.

Ridiculously he turned to the beautiful young creature in front of him who had also gained her feet and said, "Your Majesty I will always be your servant."

He bowed, jumped on his bike and pedalled to the next post box. He dared not look back.

For the rest of his round he kept going over what had happened and how he could have better dealt with the situation.

He had lost a most exquisite creature before he even had given himself a chance.

For her part Sally was amazed at the cheek of this

young man and how much of a skite he was, "Post Master General indeed!"

Next day Barry was sorting out the letters placing them in order of the houses he visited when he noticed a letter to Miss Sally Parker, 62 Gravesend Street, Bathurst.

Now he had to work a ploy and gain the attention of Miss Sally so that he could be good friends with her.

"He could suggest maybe an outing to the pictures on Saturday night or a buy her lunch in Bernie's the takeaway place, or maybe not, she's probably got a boyfriend, could even be engaged, but then again he didn't recall a diamond ring, he would buy her a diamond ring and get down on one knee and…whoa your mind is racing way too fast Barry boy let's just settle for a hello and exchange of pleasantries."

As he approached number 62 Gravesend Street he could feel his heart thumping in his chest.

He looked every way possible but there was no sign of Miss Sally Parker.

He even pretended to forget a letter for number 48 and pedalled all the way back there.

On the way back he took his time but alas there was no Miss Parker.

Reluctantly and with disappointment he placed her letter in the post box and pedalled off.

This scenario was replayed all week.

On Saturday he decided to go to the milk shop by himself and pretend she would meet him there.

He ordered a chocolate milk shake and waited for the shopkeeper to make it.

She placed the stainless steel cup full of frothy milk in front of him and he thanked her.

He hoped to catch a glimpse of some lovers so he could check out what they did. This would help him to do the same when he brought Sally there.

Disappointedly he noted that the only ones who passed by only held hands.

Later he did come across a couple where the young lady rested her head on the shoulder of her beau.

He drank all the milk shake, slurping the last drops and then chastised himself for being rude.

He asked for some popcorn at the counter.

While he waited he noticed two girls walk in and there in front of him was Sally Parker.

The rest became part of the Hayden folklore.

Barry's father in the meantime became more and more solitary.

He still turned up for work every day and did a brilliant job but he preferred his own company.

Barry didn't mind all that much as he had a much more interesting life to pursue.

One day Barry arrived home to find all the furniture in the house was gone and a large brown envelope on the mantle-piece in the lounge room.

Sitting quietly in the corner of the room was his father. He had his knees bent up to his chest and his red eyes showed he had been crying.

"Son," he said to Barry, "The Hun has declared war on the motherland and as my life isn't worth anything since your mother left I'm going to join up. I've sold all the furniture and withdrawn all the money I have from the bank. I am giving you everything to start a new life. Marry your girl and make something of yourselves."

It was June 1914 when his father waved goodbye and he knew he would never see him again.

Barry married Sally and they decided to use the money to buy a property on the Richmond River.

It was a mixed farm and they raised pigs, poultry and grew corn and sugar cane.

They were learning fast and doing quite well when they got a visit from Mr Lucas-Hughes. He said he was looking for successful farmers to farm in the Daintree River area for his Australian Agriculture Group. When he outlined what he was offering and described the area they couldn't wait.

They sold up, packed up and within three weeks they were sitting on the front verandah watching the most beautiful sunset they've ever seen.

The two boys, Ginger and Burt had sat mesmerised

throughout the Barry Hayden story.

They looked across at Sally many times during the telling and could still see that beauty that Barry had seen all those years ago.

"I think it looks like a bit of shut eye might help these youngsters recover," interrupted Sally Hayden. "Come on I'll show you where you are bedding down for the next few nights."

Sally picked up the spare lantern that was near the kitchen sink and led the two youths towards the bedrooms.

Two neatly made beds were in the room they entered.

Sally turned to them and explained, "We have four boys all who have gone away to further their education. The Daintree has a small school but only goes up to year 6. After that students are sent away to high schools in other parts of other states. My three youngest stay with my mother and father at Bathurst and attend the local high school. Our eldest, Douglas, attends Sydney University and stays on the campus. This is Douglas and Billy's room and it is vacant for most of the year except school holidays."

She placed the lamp on the dresser then added, "The bathroom is next door to the right and the toilet is way down the back. Be careful of the steps from the back door they are quite steep. Anything else you need let us know. Make yourselves at home."

With that invitation she left them and returned to the kitchen.

The two men had moved on to farming and Barry Hayden was explaining how he moved his cream across the river to the Butter Factory, "You will need to teach all your children how to row a flattie. We move the milk in ten gallon cans by flattie and the young ones take it when they go to school. They also need to know how to swim as it is easy to fall out of boats."

Burton saw Sally returning so politely cut the conversation short, "I think I'll go off to bed now. We need to talk some more Barry as you have a lot of experience living and farming here and I need to learn as much as I can. Thanks for everything you have done for me and the family so far."

Barry stood and gestured towards the door. "Follow me and I'll show you your room. The toilet is out the back down steps and the bathroom is to the right second door. We all have to share so give a knock before entering. Here's your room."

Here Burton saw a neat room with two beds.

On the door were two sheets of paper stuck with sticky tape. The top one read Terry, the bottom Anthony. "Our two youngest," said Barry noting Burton looking at the neatly formed lettering. "They are away in Bathurst attending school. We have two others, Douglas who goes to Sydney University and Billy. Sally's mum and dad billet the youngest three."

The room was illuminated by a lamp that glowed strongly from a settee between the head of the beds.

Barry left Burton who pushed his hands into each bed in turn, selected the one closest to the open window, sat down to untie and removed his work boots.

He pulled off his socks, blew out the lamp flame and flopped into bed.

He was dog tired and instantly fell into a deep sleep.

Chapter 34

The next morning was another of those glorious ones found on the Daintree. The sunrise was spectacular as the first rays touched the mountains and the splattering of clouds far in the distance.

Golden yellows, deep reds and soft smudges of purple came and went as the sun peeked over the horizon and finally came into full view.

The predominant colour though was red.

The girls and the two babies were up and about to watch this spectacular colour display.

Other people who stayed at the lodging house were also bustling around. The smell of burning toast and bacon frying was in the air.

"Look how blue the sky is mum," said Madeline.

"And the breeze is so gentle and cool," added Eva as she picked up Keith and took him into the eating area of the Lodge.

All the others followed with Marion at the rear carrying baby Max.

They selected a table that had already been set and sat down. Everyone was looking forward to a hearty breakfast as they had big plans for the day.

A middle aged woman came from the kitchen and loudly introduced herself, "I'm Maggie and I will assume you all want toast, bacon and fried eggs and a glass of milk. Any variation will cost three pence."

"That sounds fine, said Marion. "We are the Johnson family and will be farming up the Stewart Creek."

"I know who you are lovey, make it my business to know who comes and goes in the Daintree. Not big so it's fairly easy except for the itinerant and swaggies who come and go like boogies in the night."

"Could I ask for toast only for Keith here, thanks and I'll wait for the children to eat before I order."

Again Marion was showing her, 'waste not want not,' attitude of mothers of the time.

The bacon and eggs arrived and the girls gasped at the size of the serving. There were three rashers of bacon fried to crackling stage, two fried eggs – well done and two pieces of toast.

"This will take me all day to eat," said Eva.

"You and me, both," agreed Madeline.

Isobel said little but tucked in delirious at the amount and how it was cooked to her perfection.

Marion said, "Eat as much as you can we have a big day ahead. Anything you don't want you can move it to my plate."

Marion ended up with more than any one of the others and everyone ended up satisfied.

They thanked Maggie for the lovely breakfast and

then pushed in their chairs before trooping outside.

The sun was higher in the sky and was a fiery ball against the azure sky. The clouds they saw to the east earlier were still there.

"Our day will be exploring the town and walking along the track towards Stewart Creek. If we are lucky we might be able to see the farm and house we are going to live in."

"Why can't we go there now, mum?" asked Isobel.

"Well the last people to live there left the Daintree about eight months ago and it has been vacant all that time. Some strangers squatted in the house and by the time Mr Lucas-Hughes discovered them it was a mess. He has had his workmen up there getting it up to standard so we can live in it."

"So how long will it be before we can move into our own place and start farming?" asked Eva, looking hopeful.

"Probably tomorrow after breakfast," came a mascu-line reply from behind them. It was Mr Lucas-Hughes himself.

He had seen the family and was making his way to give them the good news when he overheard the question from Eva.

"Oh goody," cried Eva.

"Good morning, Mr Lucas-Hughes," greeted Marion cordially. "That is indeed wonderful news. Does Burton know?"

"Yes, mam," replied Mr Lucas-Hughes, "I rode out to your farm this morning and the foreman told me he would be finished this evening. I inspected the house and surrounds and was pleasantly pleased with the quality of work. I then rode over to the Hayden's property to inform your husband of the news. They were all down at the barn finishing the milking. Burton and the two lads were lending a hand.

"Mr Hayden was suitably impressed by your husband's knowledge, skills and work ethics."

All the while he was speaking Mr Lucas-Hughes was fidgeting and moving his feet.

He was a busy man and needed to be on the go.

He worked very long hours and would be at one place one hour organising the sale of pigs, then another hour fixing a fence, onto a ferry to cross the river to inspect the abattoir and so on.

His life was frenetic and purposeful.

"Will be off," he said, touched his broad brimmed hat and strode away from the family.

The family bade farewell and went off in search of the Butter Factory manager. They were hoping to find Mr Bryan Poole who had taken charge only last month.

As they entered the large doorway a cheery voice called, "Hello folks, my name's Bryan Poole, be with you in a minute."

True to his word a head popped around a corner of

a huge silver vat and another cheery call, "Welcome to the Daintree and to the centre of the universe. Without this factory all around you would have remained wooded and silent of human habitation."

"Good morning," said Marion, "I'm Marion Johnson and these are my children, Madeline, Eva, Isobel, Keith and the baby is Max."

Each child nodded at the mention of their name and it wasn't long before Bryan Poole was calling them by name.

"Let me explain how our set up works. Keith, where does the milk come from?"

"Cows, sir," replied Keith almost too eagerly.

"Correct, and while I've got your clever mind at work, and who keeps and milks the cows?"

"My dad," said Keith.

"Bright boy you have their Mrs Johnson. "Now Isobel how does the milk get to the factory on the Daintree?" asked Bryan Poole.

"I'm not really sure but I would guess by boats on the river."

"That's a good answer. All our cream is rowed over in flatties, the little rowboats you would have seen on the beach when you arrived yesterday. The dairymen put their cream into the ten gallon cans you see over there," Bryan Poole pointed to a whole lot of cans sitting lopsided near the bottom of a ramp outside the door they had entered.

"Most of the children going to school row them over and we help them up the slope using a horse and slide. The horse at the moment is having a smoko, I mean a rest around the back in the stables. The slide is that contraption you can see just past the cans."

"Do we have to learn to row a boat?" asked Eva and she screwed up her nose.

"I'm afraid so and you will also have to be strong swimmers if you are going to stay in the Daintree. You will soon find out that nothing moves very far here unless by waterways," declared Bryan Poole.

"This could be fun Eva, all the time in the water learning to swim and row. Will beat the heat that seems to be building," said Madeline.

"Gets very hot out here at times and you will find everyone will go off to the pool down where the Douglas and Stewart Creeks converge. Lots of fun for everyone, including the ladies," said Bryan Poole.

"Now where was I, oh yes as farmers you will milk the cows and then separate the cream from the milk leaving skimmed milk. Most of the farmers here use the skimmed milk for the family and feed the rest to pigs. Once the cream is here we weigh and grade it before putting it in this huge churn. We have two churns in the factory as we are expecting an increase in the production of cream over the next twelve months," continued Bryan Poole.

"Yes," said Marion, "We've all spent plenty of time on the handle of the separator, whizzing the milk around until we have the cream run off leaving just the skim milk."

"We have a steam engine doing the work here. We use the wood from the saw mill next door to keep the boiler going. Once we've got the cream into the churn we start beating it and slowly it will coagulate and turn into lovely yellowy butter. We put this into large packing cases wrapped in grease proof paper. These are sent downstream to Port Douglas then further south to packing factories in Cairns and Brisbane. They process the butter into the one pound butter blocks you buy at the shop," explained Bryan Poole.

Bryan Poole opened the churn and out flowed the butter into a holding bowl.

He used a large wooden ladle to collect the butter that clung to the sides of the churn.

He stopped when all the butter had been removed and put the oversized ladle down.

He took a piece of grease proof paper, scooped up a handful of butter and slapped it on the paper.

He wrapped the butter up and handed it to Marion, "There Mrs Johnson, a sample of the finest butter in the World, I'm sure you will appreciate that in the coming days."

"Thank you," replied Marion as she received the package. "And thank you for the tour it has been most enlightening. Come along everyone we'll go next door to look at the saw mill."

"I don't like that buzzing noise," complained Isobel, "It hurts my ears. I've been hearing it since I woke up."

"That is the saw biting into the log, the harder the timber the higher the pitch." Mr Edward Hitch was explaining how the saw mill operated. "Most of our timber is local with farmers cutting down the scrub and then floating the logs down to here. We cut the timber to lengths, widths and thicknesses that the locals want and the off-cuts are thrown onto the heap next door for the boiler at the Butter Factory. We use steam to drive our engine that drives the saw."

A huge log went thumping onto a flat bed and two men lined the log up and one pushed a lever to hold it in place.

They began to push the log along on rails towards a huge saw that was spinning ferociously ahead.

As the log met the saw the pitch of the noise changed and there was sawdust flying in all directions. Most landed and fell into a pit beneath the flat bed.

The screaming of the saw as it chewed through the timber sounded like the log was calling for help.

They all pushed their palms onto their ears and waited for the saw to finish its journey along the log.

They watched as a thin slice of wood fell from the log.

They observed the two men pulling the log back to its starting point before one adjusted the clamping lever and the process began again.

"This goes on all day, every day as long as we have timber," said Edward Hitch. "Tell your husband if he ever needs any timber for fence posts, pigsty fences, barn walls, telephone posts or making furniture he can get it here."

He spoke quickly getting his message across in between the screaming of the saw.

"Can we go now please mum?" shouted Eva, "My ears are beginning to hurt."

"Thank you Mr Hitch," said Marion as she shepherded the children out the door into a quieter zone.

They all walked relieved towards the Lodging House.

They were just in time for lunch and were delighted to find a round of curried egg sandwiches waiting on the table they occupied yesterday.

There was a glass of milk for each of them and then Maggie appeared to tell them that she had made a batch of scones and she was happy to give them each one with plum jam.

"Yummy," said Madeline.

"We'll wait and see if you can eat what's in front of you before we look to special treats," said Marion.

The children had had an interesting and informative morning and they were rather peckish.

The sandwiches and milk disappeared and the scones were soon following.

Marion went off to discretely feed Max.

When she returned Max delighted his siblings with a loud display of burps and blew bubbles.

Chapter 35

The family sat on the verandah of the lodge taking in the beautiful sunny sky and relaxing.

"And what are you thinking of doing with yourselves this afternoon?" asked Maggie as she began to collect their dirty dishes and clean up.

"I thought we could walk along the track that runs close to the Stewart Creek. I believe it is only about four miles to where our new farm is located. Is it easy to find?"

Maggie stopped what she was doing and hesitated for a moment. There was something left unsaid before she caught herself and said, "It's an easy walk but I'm not too sure about taking the baby. He will be quite heavy and that will tire you out"

"It will be fine, thanks Maggie. The girls are a great help and we can share the baby around. He's always been pretty good and once you start a rocking motion he sleeps like a tot."

"It is only one track wide and cuts through thick scrub. It was made for riding horses in single file. As it has been dry the last few weeks it will be an easy walk. You go along past the buildings and turn right," said Maggie.

She was happy to give the clearest of instructions

as she had seen too many newcomers come unstuck in the rainforest.

Maggie continued, "A short road turns into a track. Just follow that and you will see the Stewart Creek on your right. You will need to be back well before sundown as it is impossible to see where you are going in the dark and with the forest canopy closed over you. If you're not back by four I'll send my Jim for you."

"Thank you, Maggie," said Marion.

She looked at the woman and felt there was something she wasn't telling them. "Is there anything else we should know?"

"Well," began Maggie, then again she hesitated and went on, "Now that will be all, just be back by four."

The family went to collect their head gear ready for the walk.

The girls all had their bonnets on and Keith had a hat that was second-hand from Burt. It was brown felt with a brim.

Marion had asked Maggie for a hessian water bottle so that they could quench their thirst on the walk.

Maggie obliged and the bag was now dangling across Marion's right shoulder. Max was in a sling under her left arm.

They walked and chattered and pointed excitedly to all the unusual things they saw.

For the first mile and a half it was easy going with

sparse scrub and open areas where the timber cutters of last century had denuded the landscape in their hunt for the valuable red cedar trees.

The track entered a thick forested area where the tangle of vines, trees and shrubs were close on either side. The sun was not able to penetrate the thick overhead canopy. It was gloomy but refreshingly cool as the family trudged along.

Every now and again they would stop as one the group would excitedly point out the calling of a bird. No matter how hard they searched no one saw the bird.

As they continued they caught glimpses of the Stewart Creek running idly on their right. Sometimes they could hear the water cascading gently over rapids.

They took it in turns to share the burden of the baby and the water bag. The latter got lighter as they drank from it to quench their thirsts.

Finally they emerged from the jungle like environment and in front of them was a wide pool of water and on the far side to them was a wide expanse of golden brown sand.

"Look at that beach," shouted Eva, "Can we go for a paddle mum?"

A nod was enough and she squealed with delight, "Shoes off, socks off, last one in is…" said Eva but didn't get time to finish as she noted everyone else was running and she was left behind.

"Not fair, not fair you haven't taken off the foot-wear," complained Eva.

As she continued to protest Madeline began to kick water at her and soon she joined in the frolicking.

Marion sat down on the beach under the shade of a tree growing on the creek bank.

She was pleased to have made it this far and to be able to take the load off her aching feet.

She nestled Max into her lap and called to Madeline to look after Keith. He was already up to his knees and having a fun time sweeping the water with both hands and directing the water at his sisters.

Marion must have dozed because she was startled by a different sound to what she had heard since arriving in the Daintree. The children were still in almost the same place as she recalled they were so her shut eye could not have been too long.

Unconsciously she looked up to check the angle of the sun which would allow her to determine the approximate time. She was remarkably accurate and had improved over the years she had used this method.

Sometimes she wished she could afford one of those lovely gold watches but that wasn't possible at the moment.

She was surprised to see that the once brilliant blue sky was full of grey clouds all racing in different directions.

It was mesmerising to watch as they scurried to the west and south. It actually looked like there were two layers.

She turned back to the children and was about to call them to go back when the first thunder clap rolled over the valley.

"Come on we've got to head back it looks like a storm is coming," called Marion.

Everyone rushed from the water, gathered their shoes and socks and began to put them on.

Marion busied herself with Max and the water bag.

She was fussing around and urging them to move along when she noticed the circles forming on the still water of the lagoon the children had been playing in. At first there was a few then more and more until she felt a drenching rain hammering down on them.

She ran for the shelter of the trees where the track entered the forest.

They huddled together, dry at first, but as the rain continued to pelt down and the thunder claps increased in loudness and intensity, the fall through started to soak them all. The rain was torrential and went on and on and there seemed no end to the down pour.

Wet, tired, shaken and confused, Marion finally said, "There's nothing else for it children, we start walking."

She knew that nightfall was coming on and the

storm had blotted out the sun making it likely darkness would be upon them earlier than usual.

They had walked almost all the way through the gloomy scrub when Madeline cried out, "Stop, there's a gushing of water ahead. Sounds like a tremendous waterfall."

The extra water that was falling across the entire Daintree Valley was building up quickly and causing localised flooding.

The Stewart Creek was bulging at the banks trying to cope and get the water into the wider, deeper Daintree River.

In the meantime the tide had begun to run up the river adding more water to the already overflowing creeks.

Ahead of them, where they had heard the rapids, the family found the creek had burst its banks and was rapidly rising across the track that they had to use to get back to the Daintree Village.

The force of the water was far too great for them to wade through and besides it was rising so rapidly that it would be over their heads shortly. Even where they stood water was starting to flow by.

"Quick, follow me," called Marion and she struck out to the right running at ninety degrees to the track, searching for higher ground.

Everyone knew this was a dangerous thing to do.

However it was being swept away in a flood versus

becoming lost in the jungle like environment.

It was hard work pushing through the entangled undergrowth.

Marion was in front carrying Max and had somehow found Keith's hand and he was trailing behind but clinging tight.

The three girls had sensibly joined hands and were keeping up with their mother's furious pace.

For some inexplicable reason Marion changed course after about thirty yards.

She turned left at a right angle to the direction they were originally on.

This lined the group up parallel to the Stewart Creek Track. Whether it was because the rushing water sound had receded and she felt she had her bearing to town correct no one knew.

Within twenty minutes of the manoeuvre they burst out of the forest and there before them was open grassland. They were scratched and bruised but luckily had avoided the ghastly stinging nettles that they had heard about.

They were all soaking wet but greatly relieved by the change in scenery and the relative safety they now found themselves in.

Half an hour later Isobel was the first to hear the noise that had bugged her all morning. She was so excited she yelled, "It's the saw mill, I can hear the saw mill, oh what a wonderful sound." Everyone started laughing.

It was a wet rabble that joyously entered the Lodging House still laughing from Isobel's change of mind about the saw mill noise.

Maggie was shocked and started fussing around them all organising hot baths and clean towels.

After they all had settled Maggie came over to Marion who was sitting in a comfortable chair in the eating area and sat down.

"I must apologise to you Marion," she said using the Christian name as a show of friendship.

"No it was my silly fault. Whatever was I thinking taking the children on such a long walk in a place that is still foreign to us all. We certainly have learnt a lot of lessons this day."

Maggie looked at Marion and said, "When you have been around these parts for a few months you will be a seasoned Daintree person and the warning signs will flash in big letters. You see I knew it was going to rain late this afternoon because I saw the warning signs this morning. I was going to tell you at lunch but you all seemed so excited about walking the Stewart Creek track and I thought you would be back before the rain came that I decided not to say anything."

"How did you know about the storm?" asked Marion hoping to learn her first lesson on Daintree warning signs.

"Did you see this morning's sunrise? Well there is a very true saying that goes;

'Red sky at night
is a shepherd's delight,
red sky in the morning
is a shepherd's warning'.

And this morning the sunrise was spectacularly red."

Chapter 36

Burton was finishing breakfast when the telephone rang three times and stopped. It rang three more times and again stopped.

Sally lifted the receiver from its cradle and held it to her ear.

She stood on tip toes and spoke into the speaker on the wall. "Sal here, who do you want?"

Three things stuck Burton as he listened. First was the fact that the Daintree had telephones out on the farms, second they were party lines hence the ringing signal and thirdly the no nonsense way the Daintree folk dealt with everyday life.

"Burton it's Mr Lucas-Hughes for you,' said Sally shaking the receiver in his direction.

Burton stood up and walked around the table to take the receiver.

"Hello Mr Lucas-Hughes," he called loudly.

"I arranged for a dozen head of cattle to be on your farm yesterday. They'll need milking this morning. Give Barry a hand with his work and then ask him to show you the ropes. Tell him I'll be in debt to him. Bye."

"There it was again," thought Burton as he tried to replace the receiver and missed the silver cradle.

The telephone clattered loudly against the wall.

Sally swiftly retrieved it and hung it up saying, "Happens all the time I'll be glad when we get one of those new-fangled ones."

Burton called the two boys and they headed down to the Hayden's barn. Barry had left earlier, even before the sun was up.

He had forty cows to milk. Two hired hands were busy squeezing the teats and watching the milk spray into the pails between their legs as the trio approached.

"Mr Lucas-Hughes buzzed," said Burton, "Asked us to give you a hand and then begged you to give us a hand. Said he'd owe you one."

"Thanks will be obliged. Grab a stool, pail and I'll send a cow around, only four to go. This here's Bob and Sue married and good workers. And this here's Burton and his boys Burt and Ginger. Give you a guess who's who."

He chuckled at his own joke as everyone nodded to each other.

The milking didn't pause even for a second.

Two cows appeared with Barry encouraging them to move along by touching them on the rump with a long cane of Lawyer's Grass.

'Did you get to see the sunrise this morning," asked Barry to no one in particular, "Reddest sky I've seen for a while so expect the unexpected. By four this afternoon my best guess is it will bucket down with a few claps of thunder. Any way we take no chances. Bob and Sue will do the separating and take the cream across to Burton's barn. They can collect your cans and take them into town. We'll mosey over to your place and find the cows and milk them. Lucas-Hughes had them delivered yesterday to the bottom paddock.

"When we've finished we'll move your herd up onto the high ground near your house. You have about the highest house above the flood plain of everyone on the Daintree. We'll move my herd now as we go so that if there is a flood coming they should be out of reach."

The cattle that were to form Burton's herd were scattered across the valley between the Douglas Creek and the Stewart Creek.

One had managed to wander further afield than the rest and had crossed the Stewart Creek to the greener grass on the other side.

It took half an hour to get eleven into the barn and start the milking.

Barry left the three Johnson's busily milking while he set off in search of number twelve.

He walked along and every so often would stop and cup his hands to form a trumpet shape. He would put this to his mouth and call a low loud drawn out, "Come on." This sounded like a cow lowing to its mates.

After fifteen minutes Barry heard a familiar call coming from across the creek.

He put his right hand to his forehead to shade his eyes. Sure enough he could make out the silhouette of a cow behind bushes across the creek and a wide sand bar.

He cupped the hands and began to call continuously.

The cow came walking out of the scrub, splashed across the wide, shallow water and trundled up to Barry.

"Bit late Strawberry, old girl," he said jovially and whacked her on the rump with the Lawyer cane.

"No more across the creek or you'll get gobbled up by a croc or washed away in a flash flood. You should know better."

Barry untied the cord he had on his belt and dropped it over the cow's head. He tied it at the throat and used the trailing rope as a lead. This way she would know where to go in future.

Burton was still scratching his head and looking to the horizon for the storm that was supposed to beset them.

So far all he could see was wispy white clouds to the east and a beautiful azure sky.

One of nature's finest days where you love to be alive.

Barry had suggested they all go up to the house that would become the Johnson abode so that he could show them around.

Once this was done he believed they could move in and get started on running a successful dairy farm.

He showed them where the vegetable patch used to be, the remnants of an orchard, a broken down pigsty and the house itself. All the while he was being shown around Burton was planning.

It was getting late and the clouds had been building. The rate the clouds came tumbling from the east and south surprised them all.

"Is this your storm you predicted?" asked Burton as they arrived at the farmhouse.

Barry replied, "The same one and you can see how quickly conditions can change here. I remember about four years ago we were walking across the lower paddock about ten yards from the creek. Nothing in the sky above, a few clouds over the mountains to the west, the next thing a wall of water proceeded by logs, vegetation, mud you name it came roaring at us. We ran uphill like we were being chased by demons. Luckily we got to a fallen down tree and scampered up the trunk. It had fallen onto one of its thickest branches so it was eight feet off the ground at its highest point. The water roared around us for sixteen hours leaving a foot to spare. It was a flash flood that had started from torrential rain 100 mile away on the mountains. Never trust anything and be aware of the warning signs. This coming storm could be a blinder too or a fizzog. Doesn't matter which, get yourself, family and cows to higher ground."

The rain and thunder began just after five o'clock. "I hope Marion and the children are safe and sound," said Burton.

The rain stopped during the night and the day dawned bright and humid. Barry was up and readying to go to milk the cows when Burton entered the kitchen.

"Toast and bacon and eggs are on the stove, help yourself. It looks like we're in for a typical Daintree day, very muggy."

"How's the creek height?' asked Burton. They had sat on the verandah until nightfall watching the Douglas Creek rise and flow over its embankment. The creek continued to rise until they could no longer make out the edge of the creeping water. They had all retired hoping that the rain would cease and the water would subside. According to Barry this would happen rapidly because the Daintree River was wide enough to take the extra volume and flush the water out to sea.

"Creek's dropped back to its banks so there's good news. If you three help me with the milking I'll lend you a hand. Bob and Sue can deliver the cream; they're experienced enough to row through the flooded areas. Then we can get you settled in and let your wife know that we'll pick her up this afternoon," suggested Barry.

"Sounds like a plan to me," replied Burton as he dished up a plate of bacon and eggs. He added the same onto two other plates just as Burt and Ginger entered the room.

"Come on eat up, plenty to do today and by night we'll be in our own home."

Burton, Burt and Ginger rowed into town with Bob and Sue Walters. They had a small house in Daintree near the school.

There were two flatties directly down from Hayden's barn on the sand bank of the Douglas Creek.

The section of water from here to the Stewart was navigable but any further up was too shallow.

They loaded the cans full of cream into the flatties.

Bob started rowing one of the boats and Sue the other.

Burton sat in the rear looking at Sue and his two cans of cream. He was immensely proud today because he could make out the BBJ label on the cans.

Burt and Ginger sat in the other flattie with Barry's cream cans.

Bob was demonstrating how to row so that at every stroke the little boat shot forward and then eased as he lifted the oars and brought them back through the air before dipping them once again. The rowlocks he explained were important to keep the oars in position and in the boat.

As they swept out into the deeper, wider Stewart Creek, Bob called out, "Okay you rookies time to learn to row, swap places."

Burton was surprisingly adept at rowing then he told them he used to be in the school rowing team at Murwillumbah. He rowed the Tweed River for nearly eight months until the boat sank and the school couldn't afford a new one.

Burt was a beginner and spent more times 'catching a crab' and so his flattie was left behind in the race to the jetty.

Once Ginger took over positions closed rapidly. He pretended to be a learner at first but then told them the story of his earlier years on the canal in England.

"When I was in my teens in England I found an old boat on the bank of a canal near where I lived with my sponsor, Mr Frisworth. It was a wooden boat with three large holes in the bottom. I dragged it out of the canal and left it to dry in the sun. I scrapped out all the dried mud and vegetation before towing it back using the horse to Mr Frisworth's barn. Here I spent copious hours taking out the broken planks and fitting new ones. I found some tar that I melted and smeared across the joints effectively making them water tight. For oars I took two pieces of four by one and using a tomahawk had shaped them. My first go on the canal resulted in a near drowning and several capsizes. Eventually I got the hang of rowing and spent many a lazy hour rowing up and down and across the canal."

As he related the story he grew strong and more skilled.

He rapidly gained on Burton who was ahead and determined to win the race to the jetty.

Ginger continued his story, "One day I arrived to find the boat was missing. That was the end of my rowing days but I never forgot the skills I had acquired. Now I'm on the Daintree River twelve thousand miles from my old country, rowing like crazy and shortening the gap between our two flatties. You're about to be swamped," he called to Burton as he came within three lengths.

The jetty was too close and Burton triumphantly touched in and raised his brawny fist to the sky.

"Winner," he shouted. Everyone laughed and Sue and Bob began to clap.

"Most impressed by the rowing prowess of our visitors," said Bob. "Now it's your turn to teach the rest of the family. And remember make sure they can all swim we don't want anyone drowning here."

The cream was deposited with Bryan Poole who chalked up the two cans under the name Burton Johnson.

They returned to the jetty and he and the two boys took one of the flatties and rowed back to the Hayden's farm.

The sun was passed its zenith when the men reached the Johnson farm house.

They set to tidying up and arranging the furniture

that Mr Lucas-Hughes had had delivered by launch yesterday morning. They found a supply of essentials such as vegetables, meat, canned beans, spam, eggs, bread and the like.

"The man doesn't miss much in his planning does he?" said Burton.

"He's a good man to have on your side that's for sure. You be true to him and he'll see you right every time. Need anything just call him and it will be done," agreed Barry.

"I think we are ready to get the others home and settled in. How's the river level looking, Barry?" asked Burton.

"All clear from what I can see, even the Stewart Creek has come back to normal so the launch should be able to deliver them right to the doorstep so to speak," said Barry.

He walked over to where the telephone was attached to the wall. He lifted the receiver and wound the handle vigorously. "Barry Hayden here can you put me through to the Lodge, it's 22."

He waited patiently and then spoke again, "Maggie it's Barry Hayden, can you give Mrs Johnson her coming home orders? I'll have the launch ready to roll in half an hour."

He pushed the cradle down and let it spring back up, he repeated that manoeuvre and then spoke into the receiver, "Barry Hayden again, yes I've finished with Maggie now I need to speak to Charley Morrish on number 13."

He waited again for a short period and then began speaking, "Charley, it's Barry Hayden, we are all ready at the Johnson place. Mrs Johnson will be at the jetty in half an hour, thanks, bye."

He put the receiver back in its cradle and wandered over to where the others were sitting. "All arranged you'll be in by dusk guaranteed."

"I'm amazed at how you all work out here," said Burton, "Everyone is fully primed to the plan and it is executed without any fuss. Amazing. Thanks so much for everything."

"You'll be thanking me a lot more times in the future and me you I can assure you. We have learnt that we all work together as one community or else we perish."

As Barry Hayden predicted the Johnsons were all together in their own house by dusk.

Burt and Ginger set the Meters stove and had it had burning fiercely by the time the launch had journeyed up the Stewart Creek with the others.

What had shocked Marion as they pulled onto the bank was that they were sitting in the pool that the children had bathed in just before the storm of yesterday. It was an easy four hundred yard walk up a slight slope to the house.

Marion was pleased to find the stove blazing away and she set about making a substantial stew. It was enough to last for three days.

Burton was shocked and concerned when Marion related the family's scary adventure walking along the Stewart Creek but had to agree it was the only way they were going to be able to learn to survive in this beautiful but at times terrifying environment.

Chapter 37

After a hearty meal the family moved to the verandah.

The sun was setting over the mountains to the west displaying an array of ever changing, beautiful colours.

"Isn't this just wonderful," said Burton. "Our own home at last. What do you all think the future holds for us here?"

He looked from Marion and then to each of the children as they pondered his question.

Isobel broke the silence saying, "Riches."

Madeline chimed in, "Healthiness."

Eva said, "Fun."

George said, "Family and togetherness. I've finally got myself a real family."

Burt said, "Hard work."

Keith ran to his father and said, "Scary."

Max babbled and blew bubbles.

Marion summed it all up, "Our future together will be what the good Lord intends."

"Amen," they chorused.

Afterword

What will the family experience in the wilderness where dangers lurk? Where life can be full of beauty and wonder?

In the follow-up book, you will share the lives of each of the family as they work and play for a decade in the Daintree.

Daintree Reflections

Their trials, tribulations and stories will enthral you as the Johnson family eke out an existence over the years 1926 to 1936.

They had to live through the Great Depression, the 1934 Cyclone, numerous floods and the untimely death of one of the family.

You will learn to admire this truly remarkable family and young Ginger and the camaraderie they built.

Based on real people who lived in the Daintree for a decade.

Acknowledgments

My special thanks to my partner Deborah Johnson who inspired me to write and gave me the interest in the story Daintree Destination. These people in the story are her ancestors. She has been at my side as we followed in the footsteps of Marion and Burton Johnson and their family. Starting in northern New South Wales we followed them into the Daintree. Deborah has also been photographer, editor and offered ideas and changes throughout the writing process.

I also acknowledge the following for their assistance Heather Muttimer from the Daylesford Historical Society who helped with research of the Johnson family, Tyalgum community for being so welcoming when we visited, Murwillumbah community for showing kindness as we visited sights associated with the story, Cairns Historical Society for offering to help us in our research, Daintree School and community for their hospitality, Trove as a treasure chest of old newspapers that holds so much of our history and Ancestry.com for giving me the framework for research into my partner's ancestry.

About the Author

Anthony Buirchell was born in Kojonup, West Australia in 1949.

He worked on the 'Wheat Bins' during Christmas holidays to pay his way through high school and college.

Anthony was the Head Boy of Kojonup JHS in 1964 and again at Katanning SHS in 1966.

After studying at Claremont Teachers' College he graduated and taught for 45 years in large primary schools and as a Principal in small country schools.

Through part time studies he attained a Bachelor of Social Science at Curtin University and a Bachelor of Education at Murdoch University.

He has a daughter, Stephanie and two grandsons, Kale and Dylan.

His partner is Deborah Johnson and she was the inspiration for his first book ***The Restless Immigrants: The Johnson Family***. *Blog:* www.anthonybuirchell.com